A.G.	_____	M.L.	_____
Ans	_____	MLW	_____
Bev	_____	Mt.Pl	_____
C.C.	_____	NLM	_____
C.P.	_____	Ott	_____
Dick	_____	PC	_____
EC.H.	_____	PH	_____
EC.S.	_____	P.P.	8/03
Gar	12/03	Pion.P.	10/09
Gar.U.Pl.	_____	Q.A.	5/09
G.H.	_____	Riv	_____
GRM	_____	Ross	10/09 Ann
GSA	_____	S.C.	_____
GSP	_____	St.A.	_____
G.V.	_____	St.J	_____
Har	7/26 Booai	St.Joa	_____
JPCP	_____	St.M.	_____
Jub	2/07	Sgt	_____
KEN	_____	T.H.	_____
K.L.	11/03 (Uruet	T.M.	_____
K.M.	1/07	T.T.	_____
L.H.	_____	Ven	_____
L.O.	_____	Vets	_____
Lyn	_____	VP	12/08 MULDERS
L.V.	11/06	Wed	_____
McC	_____	W.L.	_____
McG	_____		
McQ	_____		
ASH	7/07		

Close to Sunrise

Close to Sunrise

Pat Dalton

Thorndike Press • Chivers Press
Waterville, Maine USA   Bath, England

This Large Print edition is published by Thorndike Press, USA and by Chivers Press, England.

Published in 2002 in the U.S. by arrangement with Diamond Literary Agency, Inc.

Published in 2002 in the U.K. by arrangement with the author.

U.S. Hardcover 0-7862-4261-2 (Romance Series)
U.K. Hardcover 0-7540-4949-3 (Chivers Large Print)

The text of this Large Print edition is unabridged.
Other aspects of the book may vary from the original edition.

Set in 16 pt. Plantin by Al Chase.

Printed in the United States on permanent paper.

British Library Cataloguing-in-Publication Data available

Library of Congress Cataloging-in-Publication Data

Dalton, Pat.
    Close to sunrise / Pat Dalton.
        p. cm.
    ISBN 0-7862-4261-2 (lg. print : hc : alk. paper)
    1. Triangles (Interpersonal relations) — Fiction.
2. Inheritance and succession — Fiction.   3. Resorts —
Fiction.   4. Large type books.   I. Title.
PS3554.A444 C59 2002
    813'.54—dc21   2002024554

With thanks to Noni, Reinhold, Lorri, Andy, Serita, Jodi, Diane, and Linda — you each know why

Chapter 1

Her scream sliced through the steamy Florida morning.

An unknown man had invaded the bedroom while Denyse had been in the bathroom taking her morning shower. How long had he been lurking, his movements muffled by the spraying waters?

His broad back was to her and he jumped, startled by her shriek as she stepped into the bedroom. He turned. *"Whaaat — ?"*

Denyse stifled the urge to scream again. Grabbing a lamp off the desk, she brandished it with her right hand while her left hand clutched the towel tightly around her slender body.

She discovered that the lamp reached only as far as the cord stretched. Her one-handed attempts failed to dislodge the plug from the wall. Well, if she was forced to choose between her modesty and a viable weapon . . .

Her gray eyes held a glint of cold steel as she tried to sound tough. "Get out of my room!"

"Hey, hey, hold on," the intruder said, but his probing eyes suggested that he'd rather she *not* hold on. "I didn't mean to interrupt —"

"Interrupt?! What you've interrupted is your *own* continued good health if you take one step closer."

She hoped he didn't notice how her hands were trembling. She'd always felt capable of protecting herself, at a confident five-foot-eight, but he looked much taller and stronger.

"Don't panic, okay?" His tone was soft, as if he were trying to calm an irascible Doberman. "I'm sorry. I need to see Benton."

"That hardly gives you the right to just walk in here!"

She realized he probably received more than his share of invitations to ladies' bedrooms in spite of — maybe because of — his casual attire (or lack thereof). He wore no shirt, apparently not an unusual occurrence since the sun had tanned his smooth expanse of chest. His clothing consisted only of faded jeans and sneakers, no socks. She doubted that he found it necessary to force his attentions on women. But you never know . . .

Her potential assailant was already backing toward the door with his arms extended and palms spread broadly in a gesture of retreat.

Her threat to light up his life the hard way had succeeded.

A youngster totally unknown to Denyse suddenly burst into the room. His dark eyes widened when he saw her. "Oh, I am so sorry, señorita," he said, obviously startled by her appearance.

Seconds later, Carlos, the resort employee who'd transported her from Fort Myers to Sunrise Key the night before, arrived. Upon seeing her unexpected guest, Carlos smiled and greeted him jovially. "Señor Wick, you are here, good." Only then did he direct his attention to Denyse. "You screamed, señorita?" This was uttered in the same tone appropriate for "you rang?"

Denyse lowered the lamp back to the table. "Carlos, who is this man? Oh, never mind, just get him out of here!"

"No problem." The intruder's half-grin mocked Denyse, as if she were overreacting. "We'll wait for Benton at the dock."

She didn't ask what he wanted, since she didn't care to prolong the conversation while only clad in a towel. She watched as he sauntered out the door with the boy in tow.

"Carlos?" a woman's anxious voice called from the direction of the central building.

"It is all right," Carlos returned. He shrugged as if resigned to the constant hysterics of women. "I have to go explain to my wife." He disappeared before Denyse could ask for an explanation herself.

She quickly donned a wispy sundress of lime-green eyelet cotton and ran a brush through her damp auburn hair, eager to get to the dock to find out what was going on here. Her decision not to waste time with the hair dryer was wise, she confirmed as she stepped outside. The steaminess inside wasn't only from the shower; the typical atmosphere of Florida's July was pervasive.

She hurried along a path of shells to the paved area leading to the dock where they were waiting — one of only three spots on the resort to which she knew the route.

She considered it unlikely that this guy was a paying guest. Too bad, because the resort had none right now. A glimpse of his boat verified that improbability. Rather than the expensive yachts that doubtless had graced Sunrise Key's small harbor during the resort's more prosperous times, his appeared to be a fishing boat, yet sleeker than most Denyse had seen in her native New England ports.

"Not carrying a pearl-handled revolver . . . bow and arrow . . . hide-away spear?" Wick greeted. His sea-blue eyes scanned the area behind her. "Where's Benton?"

"I'm Benton," she replied with formality.

He seemed astonished to hear her claim the name. "Really?" He recovered jauntily. "And ever so much more attractive than the one I usually see." When she didn't respond, he clarified in the same humorous tone, "And need to see now . . . You know — tall, skinny man, nice tan, dark hair with dashes of silver, looks like a distinguished beachcomber . . ."

Trying to bring the image into focus in her mind, Denyse murmured, "So that's what he looked like."

"What?" As Denyse continued to concentrate on the picture Wick had evoked, he prodded, "Did you say *looked?* Past tense?"

Her affirmative nod was almost imperceptible.

"Past tense?" he repeated tentatively.

"My father died last week," Denyse confirmed softly, but without emotion.

The news appeared to stun Wick. Disbelief and grief flashed alternately on his face. He sat back on a concrete piling, deposited his chin in his hands, and rubbed both palms along his cheeks. Minutes plodded past before he spoke again. "How, when exactly?"

"Monday. Of a heart attack." She realized that she sounded as detached as a newspaper report; Wick appeared genuinely upset.

He recovered somewhat, regarding her with curiosity, "I didn't know Dennis had a daughter." When she didn't respond, he added, "He'd been in poor health for years. Too many recurrences of malaria taking their toll. You knew that, of course."

"No, I didn't." Denyse's first reaction to his look of incredulity was that she didn't owe Wick any explanations. After all, her father would have told Wick about his early marriage and daughter if he were a close friend. Yet Wick appeared so distressed by her father's death that Denyse found herself explaining, "I never knew my real father; my parents were divorced when I was only two years old. My mother remarried about a year later, and her second husband has always been my father as far as we were all concerned."

"So you never came to see him in life, but you're here like a vulture in death!" Wick spat out the comment as though he blamed her for her father's demise.

She bristled in response. "He may never have tried to see me in life, but he *did* summon me in death. He left this island and resort to me, and you're trespassing on *my* private property!"

Wick's features grew remorseful. "Hey, look, I'm sorry. I don't know why I said that. It's none of my business anyway. But your father was such a good friend, and it's such a shock . . . I was with him that whole weekend. I said 'See you next time around' to him the night before . . ."

He seemed so genuinely stricken that she couldn't remain angry. "It's okay. I guess we're both on edge."

She'd forgotten the skinny, barefoot boy in scruffy cutoff denims who'd silently blended against the neutral gray boat. Now he ran to Wick and threw his arms around his waist. "What will we do now, what will we do?" the child implored.

"It'll be all right. Like I've told you before, things work out," Wick gently but ambiguously assured him.

His son? The boy looked Hispanic, not at all resembling the person to whom he clung. Perhaps the child had inherited his appearance from his mother rather than his father. But the accent?

"How about some breakfast?" she offered. "I'd like to learn more about my father from you. My name's Denyse." She held out her hand in friendship and he grasped it longer than manners required.

"Denyse, Dennis," he said, making the

name connection between daughter and dad. He nodded toward the boy. "This is Porque, and I'm Wick, as you learned from our informal introduction in the bedroom. I'll join you, but one of us has to tend to some things on board. Porque —" He tilted his head toward the boat, and the boy scrambled back up.

Denyse felt stirrings of hostility again. What kind of man would deny a boy a nourishing, hot breakfast?

As if reading her thoughts, Wick said lightly, "There's another hand on board. The boat has a kitchen and everything. We don't usually have our meals at resorts, you know."

Denyse led the way toward the main building, as though Wick weren't far more familiar with the route than she.

"Why do you call him Porky?" she asked. "He's not exactly chubby." Maybe he'd been denying the boy meals for months and forgotten to alter his nickname.

"It's Porque." He emphasized the trilling of the "r" and the pronunciation of the last syllable as "kay."

"It's Spanish for *why* and *because,* although the former meaning is two words and the latter is one." Wick grinned. "Whybecause. Suits the boy just right. Always asking questions I don't know any better answers for." He added with sudden seriousness, "Describes some happenstances and events of his life that, too, can have no real answer."

That made her even more curious about Porque and his relationship to Wick, but he didn't volunteer additional information, and she didn't want to appear nosy.

The sound of another motor interrupted them as a cabin cruiser glided around Wick's boat and anchored on the opposite side of the pier.

"That's my brother Chad," Wick stated with an inflection of annoyance, offering no elaboration before loping back to help the cruiser tie up.

This tropical climate sure grows tall things, Denyse mused. The dark-haired newcomer towered a couple of inches above even Wick, of a leaner, yet still formidable build — at least as much as she could estimate despite his conservative attire of cream-colored slacks and chocolate brown shirt. She wondered whose bedroom he'd been in earlier this morning.

The newcomer greeted Wick with "You didn't know — ?"

"No."

"I came early to warn you —" He paused

mid-sentence, noticing Denyse for the first time, where she was concealed by the angle and shadow of Wick's boat. He continued with a stammer, "Uh, to warn you that you'd better take care of yourself now that you're another year older."

"It's not —" Wick started.

"Happy birthday!" he said heartily, slapping Wick on the back in that bizarre display of male camaraderie. He tossed a friendly grin in Denyse's direction, adding, "Get yourself a special present?"

Before Denyse could respond that she'd never been gift-wrapped in her life, Wick answered in an uncharacteristically subdued tone, "Not exactly." He gestured between them. "Denyse, meet Chad." To Chad, he explained, "It seems Denyse is Dennis's daughter."

Chad's long stride closed the gap between them in seconds. He, too, held Denyse's hand in his own strong clasp for a longer-than-necessary handshake, while eyes the color of cognac bored into hers. Florida suddenly became steamier. She felt an instant rapport with the tall, handsome stranger.

"Glad to meet you, Ms. Benton. I'm sorry about your father."

"Thank you," she acknowledged

emotionlessly. "Please call me Denyse."

"I've been awaiting your arrival. I have a business proposition to discuss with you."

Wick mumbled so softly Denyse wasn't sure if she heard correctly, "Vulture."

"We were going to the main building for breakfast, if you'd like to join us," she said to Chad.

"Love to," he replied and followed them toward the dining room.

At the end of the dock, they passed a dilapidated sign hanging limply by one hinge. Fading letters proclaimed:

SUNRISESET
LUXURY RESORT
SUNRISE KEY, FLORIDA

The splintered wood rectangle portended the condition of the entire complex from what Denyse had seen so far. At the very least, in the interest of accuracy, the word "luxury" should be crossed out.

"The resort was named Sunriseset because both sunrise and sunset can be viewed over the ocean from this island," Chad volunteered. "You can sit on the strip of beach at the south end from dawn to dusk without moving and enjoy both of Mother Nature's extravaganzas."

"That sounds lovely," Denyse answered, knowing full well that she had too much work ahead of her to sit on a beach all day. It could be a colorful, relaxing time clock for beginning and ending work, but she suspected she'd be working long into the nights, which would be nothing unusual for her — simply a change of locale. She had no idea whether that change was going to be temporary or permanent.

As they walked on, the conversation lagged until a question occurred to Denyse. "I've never understood why the islands around Florida are called the Keys."

"It's from the Spanish word *cay*, meaning island," Wick answered. "The Spanish Main originally included parts of Florida."

Chad pointed toward the land mass visible in the distance. "The island to the southeast is Captiva, so named because a famous pirate kept beautiful females captive there for his pleasure. And beyond that, connected by causeways to Captiva and the mainland, is Sanibel Island."

Captiva. Denyse saw a mental picture of voluptuous women in tattered, off-the-shoulder blouses and full skirts, presided over by a laughing pirate, who suddenly looked very much like Wick. Automatically, she cast a glare in his direction,

18

but he wasn't watching.

"Chad lives on Captiva," Wick remarked, "among other places."

Whoops. Wrong pirate. Or right pirate, wrong location. Or . . .

She forced her oddly wandering thoughts back to more mundane matters, asking, "Why didn't they run the causeway on to Sunrise Key? It's not much farther."

"Because Dennis didn't have the influence or bribe-money necessary to persuade those in power to bring it on to Sunrise Key," Wick said, scowling at Chad as if holding him responsible. "Ironically, the residents of Sanibel and Captiva were mostly opposed to the road connection. They preferred the isolation they had from being accessible only by ferry or private boat. Dennis recognized, and wanted, the additional business potential. Of course, a three-dollar toll on the Sanibel-Captiva causeway keeps out riff-raff, at least the poor riff-raff."

The trio strolled on toward the bright yellow building that rose like a sunburst in the center of the developed resort area. Scattered about the once-landscaped but now seedy-looking grounds were one-story frame buildings, a pastiche of pastel single, duplex, and quadplex cottages. They were painted the colors of sunrise and sunset, ranging from the pale blond of dawn to varying tones of pinks and peaches. The finishes, however, were filthy and peeling.

"Señor Wick, you are back!" Consuela, Carlos's wife, threw herself at Wick, giving him a motherly bear hug as they entered the dining room. She glanced at Denyse as if expecting a scolding for not comporting herself in a manner more appropriate for an employee, but no reprimand was forthcoming.

"We'd all like some breakfast, Consuela." Denyse asked her guests, "Any preferences?"

"Whatever Connie wants to fix," Wick said.

Grinning with enthusiasm, Consuela bustled her ample body toward the kitchen.

"She's delighted to have someone to cook for again besides Carlos and Jack," Wick commented.

"Jack?" Denyse questioned.

"You haven't met him yet? He's the other year-round, live-in employee. Then there's also Burt, of course, who works here year-round but has a condo on Captiva."

"I've met only Consuela and Carlos. A message was waiting for me at the airport last night telling me to take a cab to the main dock on the river, where Carlos would be waiting with a boat. We didn't arrive at Sunriseset until midnight."

Was there any moment more lonely than walking out of a plane in a strange airport with no one to greet you? Denyse wondered. Especially when two weeks sooner she might have been met by the father she'd never known. Not that he'd cared for her . . .

She determined to banish such unworthy melancholia, forcing her thoughts back to business. "What do Jack and Burt do?"

"Jack is a general handyman-type like Carlos."

"Neither of them seem to have been doing their jobs." Denyse confirmed her comment with a glance out the window.

"They can only work with the available materials," Wick defended immediately. "It's not their fault that there hasn't been enough money to keep the place up."

"Maybe you should talk to Burt about that," Chad interjected in a strange tone. "He's the accountant and office manager."

"Then I won't be needing him once I get oriented."

From behind her, a male voice with a deep southern accent disagreed. "I think you'll find this place too much to run alone, just like your father did."

She turned to confront her dissenter, a portly man in his mid-forties, who looked like a remnant of another decade. His five-o'clock shadow at nine A.M. suggested that the Burma Shave signs that had flanked some southern roads a quarter of a century ago made no impression on him, and his thinning, dark hair was pasted down stiffly. He wore faded blue jeans with a checked shirt.

"Mornin'," he greeted belatedly. "I'm Burt Johnson." He pulled out the fourth chair without waiting for an invitation.

"I'm sorry you had to hear it like that," Denyse said. "I'll give you ample notice and severance pay, of course, depending on your tenure with my father —"

"Five years I've been here," Burt interrupted. The hunch of his shoulders and his stony gaze forbade her to deny him five more.

"I'm a CPA myself, so you can understand why your services won't be needed after the transition period," she said.

She thought the hard look in his eyes was replaced by a brief flicker of fear. Then Burt stared down at the table as if stymied for an argument. Wick was grinning broadly, while Chad maintained an expression appropriate for high-stakes poker.

As she backed out of the kitchen with a tray of orange juice and coffee, Consuela declared loudly, "I fix your favorite breakfast, Señor Wick, huevos rancheros, ham, those funny potatoes — uh — hash browns —" Her exuberant chatter halted when she saw the trio had become a quartet. Setting the tray on the table with a defiant thump, she placed the glasses and cups before the original three without comment.

"I'll have breakfast, too, Consuela," Burt ordered, and selected a different menu as if deliberately complicating her cooking. "Poached eggs medium-soft, bacon, English muffin, and tea."

"You get the same as the others," Consuela said firmly, not happy to serve him even that. Denyse didn't countermand her.

She had been eager to learn more about her father from Wick, but she didn't want to make that a group discussion. And she hadn't missed the implications of that first brief exchange between Chad and Wick — the possibility that Chad had come to warn Wick about something more than advancing age. She decided to forego the usual conversational gambits, like trying to find out exactly why Chad and Wick were here, and what their relationships to her father had been.

It would probably be more interesting, and a lot more informative, to let each man reveal himself — particularly if she were alone with each of them some time soon. Somehow, being alone with either of them, especially Chad, wasn't an unpleasant prospect anyway.

Her instincts to avoid a focused discussion seemed to have been correct, since neither Wick nor Chad appeared willing to explain his reasons in front of the others for being present. Innocuous and mildly awkward chitchat was interspersed between sips of coffee and forksful of food.

Burt finished several minutes ahead of the others, having gulped his meal despite its not being what he'd ordered. He scraped his chair back as he swiped smears of Spanish sauce from the corners of his mouth. "Got to get to work."

Was he trying to impress Denyse as a dedicated go-getter, in an attempt to keep his job? Her initial impression was that his get-up-and-go got up and went years ago, if there'd ever been any at all.

Denyse halted his hasty exit. "I'd like you to show me around Sunriseset this morning."

Burt did not seem at all eager for this opportunity to ingratiate himself with his new boss. His appearance was like that of a trapped animal as his gaze bobbed round the table. "Uh, Chad can show you just as well as me. He knows all about the place."

"Sure, I'll be glad to —"

"Me, too," Wick interrupted with challenge in his tone. "I'll go along to be sure you hear both viewpoints."

"I don't understand —" Denyse started.

"You will, soon enough," Wick said.

Burt scurried out the door.

Incongruently, the two visitors conducted the owner around the resort.

Denyse had been a little mentally deflated with the harried activity of the past few days, coupled with the humid heat. Now she had the impression she was exploring a deserted 1940s movie set, escorted between a businesslike but sensual Cary Grant and a virile, bare-chested Burt Lancaster.

Paths of seashells connected the guest units with each other and with the general buildings. The interiors of the individual units weren't as run down as their exteriors indicated, no doubt preserved by non-use as well as non-exposure to the elements, Denyse decided.

The recreational facilities, though, needed to be entirely recreated. The swimming pool held slimy greenish water, and a jigsaw profusion of cracks on the bottom made the whole thing look like a giant's broken mirror, harbinger of seven lifetimes' bad luck. The concrete skin of the tennis courts was also riddled with cracks, as were the shuffleboard courts. The twin putting greens would be helpful only to a golfer planning a coup on a course of weeds.

Heading northeast from the resort, a dike of hard-packed dirt topped by the ubiquitous shells necessitated walking single file, but neither of the men started across.

Chad explained, "That leads to the bird and wildlife refuge area set aside by Dennis years ago — a lot of swamp with a few dirt trails where there are bits of solid land, and —"

"And alligators and cottonmouths and creepy-crawly things not at all of interest to a CPA from Boston," Wick continued for him. "I don't think you should risk exploring there."

Denyse had been immediately intrigued by the word "swamp." To a proper Bostonian, "swamp" conjured up misty, enticing, and mysterious images. But the fantasy was tarnished with the reality of potential encounters with slithering snakes and toothsome alligators.

As they continued on, Chad pointed out

the small generating and water treatment plants, explaining that Sunriseset functioned as a self-contained mini-community.

Eventually they arrived at the Sunset Ballroom, a large-roofed, open-air dance and entertainment pavillion. The orange paint on the half-walls was peeling and filthy, and small lights hung topsy-turvy from the ceiling on exposed cables.

"I couldn't book Dorsey here, even now," Denyse commented. "It might be perfect for a punk-rock group, though."

"Just keep those promotional ideas flowing, babe," Wick encouraged, grinning.

"About the 'babe' —" she started.

"This was quite a romantic place at one time," Chad reminisced, almost to himself. "Dennis would darken the ballroom and the tiny overhead lights would twinkle like stars in an onyx sky."

What memories lay treasured beyond those brandy-colored eyes? Denyse found herself wondering. Who had Chad romanced here? How long ago, and was she still in his life?

Within the first few seconds of meeting each of them, Denyse automatically noted that neither Chad nor Wick wore a wedding ring. But that was no guarantee of unattached status.

Great yo-ho-hos, Denyse thought. What was the matter with her? It wasn't as if she was normally a manhunter. Just because two prize specimens were within arm's reach —

Heat. It's got to be the heat, she excused herself. Her thoughts as well as her demeanor remained businesslike for the rest of their circular tour.

They wound up back at the two-story sunshine-yellow central building which contained the kitchen and dining room, along with a recreation room housing Ping-Pong, pool, and card tables. On the second floor were offices. Burt was bent diligently over a set of ledgers when they poked their heads into his office. They returned to the main floor.

The two visitors tried to outstay each other. Finally, after a glance at Wick, Chad reminded Denyse of his reason for coming. "I do have a business proposition to discuss with you."

Having been aware of Chad's physical magnetism, Denyse doubted that he was accustomed to rejections to his propositions — business or otherwise. But, not ready to contemplate buying whatever he was selling, she held up her hand in a forestalling gesture. "I'm not prepared to consider any business proposals yet. I want a

28

chance to look over the books, analyze the cash position, determine the problems —"

"Good girl!" Wick interrupted, apparently a habit of his. "I hope you'll give me a chance to state my opinion on any 'proposition' Chad or anybody else offers you."

Girl, babe . . . Wick's vocabulary definitely needed improving, Denyse determined. And he was irritatingly presumptuous in expecting to become involved in her business.

As if reading her thoughts, Wick interceded on his own behalf. "After all, I was a good friend of your father's, and I do know the resort and the area in general. Besides, I imagine Chad's proposition is the same one your father rejected many times."

"Maybe Denyse has more business sense than her father."

"Gentlemen, gentlemen. Feud if you wish, but I've got to get to work."

They both smiled, but only at her, not at each other.

An idea occurred to her. Perhaps she preferred not to spend her first full evening at Sunriseset alone, although she usually wasn't a social person. Perhaps she just didn't want to confront and dwell on confusing, unhappy thoughts of her father.

Uncharacteristically, without analyzing all the angles, she said impulsively, "What this place needs is a party. Since it's too late for the Fourth of July and too early for Christmas, I think a birthday bash is in order. How about both of you coming back tonight to celebrate Wick's birthday? Bring Porque and anybody else you want to." Wives, etcetera, she was tempted to mention, but thought such a gambit too obvious. Would Chad arrive with the dreamy partner of his bygone romantic nights in the Sunset Ballroom?

"It's not —" Wick started, and interrupted *himself* for a change. "I mean, that would be great."

"I'll be here," Chad agreed. "Let's see, Wick, whatever would you like for a present?"

The men accompanied each other out the door.

Realizing she should have asked Wick what his favorite kind of cake was, Denyse started after them. She took a shortcut across the unkempt lawn, therefore not heralding her approach with the crunch of shells on the path, and was about to skirt a huge bush with fan-like fronds to join them when she overheard, "Well now, that's what I call a *surprise* party," Wick was saying.

"What's in a date?" Chad responded. After a pause, he added, "You really shouldn't involve her, you know."

"What choice do I have? You know what I've got on that boat out there. I want a chance to size her up some more, though. We can't automatically count on her being like Dennis. Especially since she says Dennis never really knew her —"

The men's long strides took them out of earshot, leaving behind a confounded and suspicious Denyse.

She headed toward her father's office. No, it was her office now. She sat down and started to work, but with her already weary mind barraged by thoughts of her father, Wick's and Chad's remarks, and the shabby condition of the resort, it took her some time to become thoroughly immersed in her most pressing project: evaluating Sunriseset's financial position.

Finally, her inherent professionalism triumphed, and she focused her total attention on the accounting records. She had been categorized as a "single imager" when attending a biofeedback seminar a couple of years ago. Her ability to ignore all distractions, both external and internal, and concentrate wholly on the project at hand had contributed to her rapid rise with one of Boston's foremost accounting firms.

She had been among the small percentage

of students to pass all sections of the rigorous Certified Public Accountant exam immediately following college graduation. She progressed to a senior accountant position in a whirlwind three years, and had recently been promoted to audit manager, much to the distress of some of her older male colleagues. But Denyse brooked no nonsense, from herself or her colleagues, and many had come to admire her professionalism too much to allow chauvinistic attitudes to intrude.

She could probably win Burt over that same way, she knew. But it seemed pointless since she wouldn't need his services permanently.

And she certainly had no regard for Burt's accounting and administrative abilities, she confirmed to herself ruefully, while reviewing his sloppy and incomplete records. Nor could she respect her father's management capabilities, seeing that he had retained Burt and allowed a once-fine resort to fall into near ruin.

Denyse wondered from whom she had inherited her own businesslike genes. Certainly not from her sweet but sheltered mother. And, it was obvious now, not from her father. She must be some sort of mutant, she decided.

Her employer in Boston had insisted on granting her an indefinite leave of absence when her father's attorney had called regarding her unexpected inheritance.

Like many other times in the past week, Denyse felt an abrupt stab of resentment at this unknown man who died and bequeathed his entire estate to her, upsetting what had been quite a satisfactory life in Boston. For the first time in recent memory, Denyse felt unsure of herself, uncertain of her goals.

She had hoped to formulate some objectives in a few days by completing a thorough financial analysis of the resort. But she'd barely made a dent when the buzz of her alarm watch signaled the time to change clothes for the party.

Chapter 2

After a quick shower, Denyse debated how much to dress up before selecting a casual spaghetti-strapped dress with a hot-pink flowerprint splashed against a background of white.

Entering the dining room, Denyse saw that Carlos had festooned one corner with multi-colored balloons. While that section looked festive, the rest of the room appeared bleak and deserted by comparison.

Wick arrived first, with Porque solemnly walking beside him. The boy was either subdued by Denyse's presence or didn't know quite what to expect of a birthday party. The two were dressed identically in fresh blue jeans and plain short-sleeved white shirts — a style exhibiting Wick's muscled arms to advantage, Denyse had to admit.

Denyse was great with financial statements but felt deficient with children. Porque resisted her inadequate attempts to engage him in conversation: hello, how are you, how do you like school and what grade are you in. At first, Porque shrank partially behind Wick. Then, as if mustering his courage, he stepped beside Wick and looked Denyse straight in the eye.

"No speak *ingles* good, señorita," Porque excused himself.

His claim was greatly exaggerated, Denyse thought, having observed him speaking and seemingly understanding English very well earlier that day. "By the way, we anchored over on the opposite side of the island," Wick said. "I hope you don't mind."

"It's a free ocean."

"In some ways," was Wick's rather cryptic reply.

"I'm sure Sunrise Key doesn't have its very own three-mile limit. You can park on any wave you choose. Did you take a trail through the swamp to get here?"

He laughed. "No way. It's bad enough in the daytime, let alone when it's dark as death." Wick lowered his voice as if narrating a ghost story. "Know what's the only thing you can see at night? The red eyes of the alligators shining through the blackness."

"Sure. Alligators who've had too many martinis."

"No, really, that's how the 'gator hunters find them at night. But don't get any ideas about catching yourself a handbag, even though you no longer have to prove the alligator was trying to make a lunchbox out of you first. Until recently, alligators were an endangered species, but hunting them is legal again."

"For a year or two, until they're near extinction again."

"You got it."

Denyse noticed Porque looking at the buffet table. Uncertain how many guests Wick and Chad would bring, she'd instructed Consuela to lay out some salads, cold cuts, and varieties of bread. She'd noticed that the kitchen was well stocked despite the resort's current lack of customers. "Help yourself to the food, Porque."

The boy started toward the smorgasbord, then halted mid-step, realizing his response indicated comprehension of her offer. He looked to Wick for assistance.

"Esta bien. Come," Wick said gently.

"Porque's mother couldn't come tonight?" Denyse wondered if her question was appropriately casual.

"Porque's mother is — No, she couldn't."

Denyse felt obligated to fill the pause in conversation that followed. Again, she sounded more flippant than she felt. "Speaking of parents, you were going to tell me more about my father."

Chad's greeting rang out. "Happy birthday!"

Denyse turned eagerly to see who accompanied Chad, and found herself disturbingly pleased that he was alone. He looked stunning wearing a reversal of Wick's fashion colors, in white slacks and a teal blue shirt.

Emulating a sommelier, Chad presented a bottle of wine. "I wasn't sure whether to bring red or white, since I didn't know what kind of cake you'd be serving."

"That's Chad's motto," Wick said. "Some port in every girl."

And no doubt Wick's own lifestyle proved the cliché, Denyse thought to herself. She glanced at the buffet. "I'd say we have more than enough food for four."

"Pablo — that's my first mate — had to stay with the boat, but aren't Connie, Carl, and Jack going to join us?" Wick strode toward the kitchen without awaiting her confirmation. "I'll tell them the party's starting."

Pleased to have the three employees join them, Denyse noted how Wick nicknamed and Americanized all of them, except Porque whose nickname, at least, was as Hispanic as he was. Wick put them all on his own friendly terms. She wondered if all of them were so eager to be absorbed into this culture that they were willing to completely deny their real roots, even so far as to relinquish the names they'd identified with their entire lives. But at least they received real names — not just "babe" or "girl."

As the party proceeded pleasantly, the conversation remained light. Jack turned out to be Jacques, a congenial, articulate black man whose slight French accent also conveyed the lilt of the Caribbean. He, Carlos, and Consuela appeared fond of Wick and tolerant of Chad.

Wick proved to be a raconteur, regaling them with many interesting stories about Florida and the Caribbean without revealing much about himself. Although apparently content to be the quieter of the two this particular evening, Chad frequently displayed a good deal of intelligence and wit.

Again, the two guests tried to outstay each other. Wick finally acquiesced when Porque fell asleep in a chair; his departure cued Chad's leaving as well.

Half an hour later as she was walking to her cottage, Denyse heard the crunch of shells on an intersecting path. She had watched the visitors depart, Chad in his cabin cruiser, and Wick and Porque in a motorboat.

"Carlos? Jacques?" Denyse called into the blackness.

The figure who stopped in front of her was too tall to be either of the employees. Denyse started to run back toward the main building.

"Denyse, wait. It's me, Chad."

She turned, relieved. "I thought you left." She nearly made the mistake of saying she'd actually seen him go. In fact, she had followed the men to the dock, keeping to the soft ground rather than the noisy paths, hoping to overhear something that would clarify their mysterious earlier exchange. But the men's conversation at the far end of the pier had been brief and mumbled.

"I'm sorry I frightened you, but I want to talk with you alone. I'll walk you to your cottage."

Denyse was finding Chad's presence disquieting, once again aware of the physical attraction that this man seemed to hold for her. Or maybe it was just the unaccustomed humidity.

The heady scent of thousands of blossoms intensified as he stepped closer. When he gently took her arm, light tremors shook through her like ripples on the smooth waters. She tried to rationalize her reaction to Chad by reminding herself that she was unusually tired and vulnerable at this moment, and steeled her resolve because that was all the more reason to be wary.

"I was going for a walk along the beach," she lied.

"That sounds like a good idea."

He fell into step beside her. "The northeast beach is best for walking at night."

Moonlight waltzed across Sunrise Key, filtering through the palm fronds, causing the sands to glitter like fine silver shavings.

"There are fewer obstacles on this beach than the one to the south," Chad explained, although she didn't know what he meant. "More likelihood of stumbling or losing your balance there in the dark."

If she lost her balance in the dark with Chad, it might be emotionally comfortable to have a piece of driftwood to blame, Denyse thought irrationally. She tightened her hold on self-control.

"What did you want to talk to me about?" The question came out sharper than she'd intended.

"Did you get a chance to determine the resort's financial situation today?"

Great subject for conversation on a moonlight stroll. Her reply was more crisp than her question, this time exactly as intended. "I spent the afternoon reviewing the accounts. Of course, it'll take a few more days. I told you I'm not ready for business discussions yet." Pivoting, she started back toward her cottage.

He followed, catching up with a couple of long strides. "Sorry again."

She had the impression that apologizing to women was not a usual component of Chad's modus operandi.

"But I do have an important proposal for you," he persisted.

"Later in the week. I'll contact you when I'm prepared to listen."

He attempted light conversation on their way back, but Denyse wasn't too responsive. When they reached the pier, she said pointedly, "You don't have to walk me all the way back to the cottage."

"Of course I'll walk you back."

She heard the sound of a door closing as they came around the path. Probably Jacques. She wasn't sure which unit Jacques lived in, although Consuela and Carlos's quarters were in the central building.

Chad stood disturbingly near when they arrived at her cottage. "Could we plan on dinner Thursday, or lunch if you'd prefer? That's three days."

"I'll call on Wednesday and let you know."

41

He pulled a card from his shirt pocket. "My business and home numbers are on here."

She accepted the card without even glancing at it.

He reached out, and his finger traced a gentle yet tingling caress down her cheek. "I subscribe to the old adage of not mixing business with pleasure, Denyse. I'd like to get the business out of the way."

Then he was gone, leaving behind a certain amount of incentive to spur her through her management analysis.

She was startled as a lamp came on when she entered the cottage, then decided it was an automatic system. Then she got a full view of the room and Wick lounging on the bed.

"Touching little scene outside," Wick said. "But Chad's always been outstanding at sales pitches. That's how he made his fortune."

Denyse involuntarily looked at the card in her palm. *CTJ Associates*, it read.

She said in a controlled, matter-of-fact tone, "You have a bad habit of breaking and entering where you're uninvited and unwanted. What are you doing here, anyway? You left an hour ago, and you've got no business in my room."

"No business, true. That's Chad's area. But you said earlier that you want to know more about your father, and we've had no other chance to talk alone."

She examined the door. "How'd you get in here? I know I locked this."

"Not necessary on Sunrise Key."

"Maybe not, but it's literally a matter of life or death in Boston, and I haven't abandoned the habit. Stop dodging my question."

"I was waiting for you outside, like a proper gentlemen, when I heard Chad talking as you approached. So I used my key to come inside."

"What if Chad had come in with me?"

"Then I would have been in full retreat hiding behind the shower curtain in the bathroom."

"And if —"

"And if Chad had remained so long that he needed to take a shower here? Come on, Denyse, unless my judgment has totally failed for the first time, you're not that kind of girl."

"Woman," she amended.

"I notice you only corrected one part of my statement, so drop the act."

"And you drop the key. You're no longer welcome to enter this room whenever you feel like it."

After Wick laid the key on the nightstand, Denyse relented and directed the conversation into less sensitive areas. "Where's Porque?"

"I put him to bed, then came back in the motorboat."

"I didn't see it at the pier."

"No, I tied it up down the beach."

Wick's lifestyle no doubt commonly included sneaking around in the dark and hiding behind ladies' shower curtains, Denyse found herself thinking. His shirt was now halfway unbuttoned, again displaying his expansive muscular chest.

Besides the bathroom, her father's cottage was comprised of a single large room with a king-size bed, two plump armchairs, a desk and wooden chair, and a couple of tables. Wick sat on the bed. Denyse chose the farthest chair.

"About my father — ?"

"He was a real friend to me and a lot of other people."

This time it was she who interrupted. "That's funny, considering he deserted his own family." Oddly enough, she'd never been aware of any bitterness toward her father. He'd simply been a ghost in her early years, someone who had never really existed to her.

44

"I can't comment on that, except to say that it doesn't sound like Dennis. He must have had his reasons, but he never discussed them with me. In fact, I didn't know he had a daughter until you materialized this morning."

Wick lay back on the bed as though he was talking to a psychiatrist from the stereotypical couch, and began his monologue. "Dennis was a fine, fine man. A man of ideals and dreams — no, visions — because he took action to make his dreams come true. At least within one man's limitations."

Denyse had the impression Wick was describing not only her father, but also himself. Perhaps that was why they'd been close. Surely Wick must have been like a son to Dennis. Why had her father left his island and everything on it to a daughter he hadn't cared about, or even seen, for twenty-five of her twenty-seven years?

Wick continued. "I suppose you know Dennis was a man of the sea, served in the navy during the Korean War and for a while thereafter. Then he joined the merchant marine, and soon got promoted to first mate. Dennis had been everywhere, around the world again and again — Marseilles, Piraeus, Djibouti, Singapore, Colombo. Unfortunately, he contracted malaria somewhere along the way, a rare kind that re-curred several times throughout the years. But he was enterprising enough to make a lot of money on imports he brought back to the States, using cargo space that otherwise would've been empty."

Denyse couldn't help wondering if all her father's imports had been declared and legal.

"When Dennis came across Sunrise Key, he knew he wanted to develop this island. 'Course, except for the beaches, it was nothing but a lot of swamp and snakes and mosquitoes."

And on its way to reverting to that again if something isn't done soon, Denyse mused.

As if sensing her thoughts weren't echoing his, Wick stood up. "Just know that Dennis was a wonderful person." He started to leave.

"That's all you're going to tell me?"

"For now."

Despite her disappointment with Wick's condensed description of her father, Denyse automatically played the proper hostess, seeing Wick to the door.

He turned suddenly. His hands, strong and calloused from work, clamped her shoulders and he drew her out into the night, close to his muscled body. "Watch out for Chad."

Before she could protest or demand a viable explanation, Wick kissed her firmly on the lips, stepped back, and speculated rakishly, "I doubt, Miss Benton, that there have been enough swashbucklers in your life." He disappeared into a night as dark as Blackbeard's whiskers.

Denyse wandered back into her room. Wick's touch didn't excite her the way Chad's had. She ruminated on Wick for a moment. Who was Porque's mother, why was Wick looking after him?

In any case, the social prospects seemed far more promising than anticipated for a tiny island with a population of four.

Last night, she'd been too tired to ponder her situation. But tonight, Denyse's attempts to sleep were halfhearted. It felt strange to occupy the same bed, the same cottage, that had once belonged to the biological father she'd never known.

Chapter 3

Denyse rose early the next morning and decided to take a walk on the beach. She felt guilty as more shells crunched beneath her sandals, their fragile beauty destroyed forever. But there was no avoiding it. The entire beach was covered in shells, and several yards inland more had gathered on top of each other, forming a multi-hued, three-dimensional wall, a triumphant abstract sculpted by Neptune. Among the muted tints and pastels lay pleated cockles, rosy conchs, ruffled scallops, butterfly-shaped coquinas, and pointed lavender augers. To alter any part of this mural would be as criminal as slashing a Rembrandt.

Sauntering along the island's southern beach shortly after sunrise, she understood why Chad had chosen the smooth sand of the northeastern beach last night rather than trying to maintain a firm foothold here in the dark. But her footing around Chad wasn't as firm as she'd like.

Picking up a scallop shell that was the color of a sunrise, Denyse pressed it to her ear, delighting as she had as a child at the sound of the ocean that seemed forever a spirit inside.

Burt startled her and broke the spell. "You can get the same result by cupping your hand or anything else over your ear."

Denyse dropped her hand, palming the shell and glancing at her watch. "Isn't seven A.M. awfully early for you to start work?"

"I like to get a jump on things. It wasn't me that let this island go to pot, you know." A spectre of a smug grin twisted one side of his mouth. He wandered off toward the office.

Denyse wondered how the office manager had so much work that he needed to begin this early even when the resort didn't have any guests, but as salaried staff he didn't qualify for overtime pay, so she wouldn't concern herself yet. She headed after him and settled into her office.

Denyse spent the entire morning and most of the afternoon hunched over her desk and a calculator. Consuela insisted on bringing breakfast and lunch to her office, hovering a few minutes to insure that she began eating each meal. In the late afternoon, ready for a long break, Denyse decided to explore the wildlife refuge.

Threading her way through the resort and over the dike, she selected the middle of the three narrow paths. Belatedly she realized she should have checked at the main building for a map of the refuge; surely there were some brochures for the guests. Not wanting to turn back, she decided to memorize her route so she could retrace it.

The slender trail of trampled dirt wound through thick foliage. Giant ferns grew along the path. She counted at least five different types of palms, from one growing like a giant fan out of a short trunk to lofty trees cradling coconuts at their pinnacles.

Denyse was slightly disturbed by the rustlings of unseen creatures within the mini-jungle framing the path, but the pacifying music of birds could be heard nearby.

The foliage on her left ended abruptly at an expanse of shallow water the color of strong tea. Denyse remained quiet, hoping not to frighten away the many birds wading, swimming, fishing, and soaring above — huge white herons, smaller gulls, brown ducks, and others, including a pair with broad bills and feathers of deep pink. She vowed to buy a guidebook to identify them all, or better yet, to have Chad or Wick accompany her sometime to explain them.

This scene, the complete atmosphere of this place, was tranquilizing. Denyse began to experience a sort of spiritual empathy, almost communication, with her father, and was grateful to him for preserving this little piece of the world.

Though the aura didn't seem seriously threatened when thick charcoal clouds began to overshadow the blue sky, she decided to start back.

She assumed the trail led in a circle, allowing people to explore most of the refuge without covering the same ground twice. She'd probably reach the resort faster by continuing forward rather than heading back the same way.

She underestimated the rapidity of Florida's weather change. In a few minutes, dark clouds covered the horizon, cloaking the swamp like a shroud and instantly changing the four P.M. light to dusk. The smooth water mirrored the blackness, appearing like an entrance to a murky netherworld, reflecting silhouettes of towering trees like inky renderings on slate.

The swarthy clouds seemed purposeful, as though gathering for an attack, and succeeded in altering Denyse's mood from total peacefulness to ominous foreboding.

Like phantoms, wisps of pale fog began to creep across the dark water, around the pond-cypresses and white ghost orchids.

Denyse's stroll became a jog.

She stopped short when the menacing silence was shattered by a chilling, soul-wringing cry.

She remained still for a couple of minutes, like a child playing hide-and-seek with an irascible Mother Nature. The cry was not repeated.

As she started to run again, the clouds made good on their threat. First, a single large drop of rain. Mere seconds later, a deluge. The path soon would become a mire.

She noticed a building a short distance away to her left. Scanning the path, she saw a thread of trail not quite overgrown, and eagerly detoured.

The windowless cinderblock structure was the size of an average house. A storage building, Denyse supposed, hoping it wasn't locked.

She twisted the knob, and the metal door swung open without protest. Taking only a few steps inside and partially shutting the door against the rain, she tried to see through the room's darkness.

Her foot encountered a slick wetness on the concrete floor, and suddenly she felt a sharp pain in her head. She plunged head-long into darkness.

Rocking, rocking. Mother. Yes, she must be curled in her mother's lap, rocking. A whiff of ocean air. On the bay in New England where they went that summer. Rocking on the porch in her mother's lap. Her mother gazing out to sea with a tinge of wistfulness.

"Are you awake? Are you okay?" An anxious voice. Not her mother's voice.

Denyse shifted slightly and a pain shot through the back of her head. She moaned.

"You'll be all right, I'm taking you to the hospital," the voice assured her.

Several minutes passed before Denyse attempted movement again, risking half-opened eyes. That didn't hurt too much. She opened them all the way.

And saw red. Red wavering back and forth.

It took her awhile to realize that she was looking at the sky in the blaze of sunset. And many more seconds to realize that the rocking was a motorboat on an inhospitable ocean. The voice had been Wick's.

Denyse tried to sit up, attracting Wick's attention again, along with a command. "Don't move around. I'm taking you to Cape Coral, just west of Fort Myers. We'll go up the canal nearest the hospital, where they have an ambulance waiting."

Lying back, grateful for an excuse not to stir, she managed to ask, "What happened?"

"I guess you fell or tripped on something and hit your head."

"That's right." Waves of memory began stirring in her mind. "The swamp. But how'd you know, how'd you find me?"

"I decided to have dinner with you at Sunriseset and took the trail across the swamp instead of boating. When the rain started, I headed for that old building, and there you were."

"Lucky for me you came that way . . ." She felt herself slipping back into oblivion.

Some time later, she was aware of hands lifting her. A soft bed. A beam of light shining through the darkness into her eyes, disturbing her, again and again.

The back of her head ached dully when she awakened the next day, disoriented to find herself in a strange hospital room. Looking through the window didn't tell her whether the sun was on its way up or down. Her semi-private room wasn't shared by anyone at the moment.

Hearing someone enter, Denyse rolled over. A young pant-suited nurse greeted her with a smile. "You're awake. Good."

"How am I?"

"I should be asking you that," the nurse responded. "You had a mild concussion — the result of a fall, I understand — but the

54

x-rays indicated no permanent problem. That headache you probably have should be easing up soon, but the doctor's planning to keep you here another day to play it safe."

The nurse checked her pulse, blood pressure, and eyes, while Denyse ascertained that the time was midafternoon. "You're doing fine," the nurse said.

Denyse was glad to learn that, since the pain in her head indicated otherwise.

"I guess you're set for visitors now. The hospital grapevine says this man has been waiting ever since you were brought in last night — all night." She added with a mischievous grin, while comically wiggling her eyebrows up and down, "I'd keep a gorgeous guy like that away from the nurses' station if I were you."

So Wick had waited. Somehow she hadn't thought he was the type to stay in one place that long.

"I'd like a little time to freshen up."

"Sure. Five more minutes shouldn't make much difference to him. I'll pull this curtain." The congenial nurse pulled closed the drape between the beds before she left.

As Denyse sat up, a wave of light-headedness came over her. Vanity prevailed, and she managed to find a comb in her nightstand drawer and drag it through her auburn hair.

Though she wasn't usually overly concerned about makeup, the lack of lipstick was disconcerting. Oh, well, she consoled herself. Maybe some men liked the pale look. Maybe she could develop a cough to complete the image.

Hearing the door open and close again, she pulled the bed sheet high around her neck. "Come on in, Wick."

"Sorry once again," the deep velvet voice replied. "It's Chad, not Wick." He peeked playfully around the curtain. "May I come in anyway?"

"Of course." Had it been Wick who'd remained all night, with Chad just arriving? "It's nice of you to come. How did you know?"

"Wick had the hospital call me when he radioed them. I was waiting along with the ambulance."

As he sat in the chair alongside her bed, Denyse discerned shadows beneath his eyes. "You stayed here all night?" Appreciation laced softly through her voice.

Chad shrugged his shoulders as if self-consciously shrugging off her commendation, mildly embarrassed that she'd found out. "I just wanted to be sure you were all right." He offered her a large, square box tied with a gold ribbon. "I thought you might need a few things."

"I hope you brought me a new head," she said, still aware of the ache in her own.

"It would be kind of square," he said mockingly, eyeing the shape of the box. "Would that suit you?"

"I suspect I've been called square on more than one occasion — and worse," she answered with a smile.

"If you weren't square, you could perform the Dance of the Seven Veils and demand the head of John the Baptist."

"I'm still a little too shaky to get further than one or two veils, and I wouldn't look good in a beard."

As she untied the bow, she saw the logo of the hospital gift shop on the box. Inside was a sunshine-colored silky robe in a kimono style. Denyse ran her fingers across the fabric. "It's beautiful."

Then she noticed a small jewelry box in a corner. She remembered his business proposition from earlier. Was this to pave the way for some sort of sales pitch?

"Thank you for the robe," Denyse said. Picking up the jewelry box, she added in her most prim Boston Miss manner, "But I don't know if I can accept this." If the contents were too expensive, she'd return it to him right now.

"Don't worry. I can afford it."

This was her first clue about Chad. Was he accustomed to buying women with expensive baubles?

"Whether or not you can afford it isn't the point."

"I suspect that once you take a look inside the box you'll decide to keep it." He turned on a grin as dazzling as the Hope Diamond.

It was kind of fun, possibly being plied with jewelry, even if it were soon-to-be-returned jewelry. She'd only seen that happen to women in vintage movies on television. Usually, the recipient was an actress and the male bestower referred to as a stage-door Johnnie. She'd never seen a movie where the characters were a Certified Public Accountant and a hospital-door Chad.

A glint of gold caught the light as she lifted the lid of the box.

A lot of gold.

"A tube of lipstick!" she exclaimed.

"I'll take it back if you want," Chad teased, "but I think I'd look awful in that color."

They laughed together.

"I think it's called something like Pink

Pearl, so the jewelry box wasn't totally inappropriate. There are a few other essentials under the robe — hairbrush, a toothbrush, stuff like that."

"Great. Thanks again." Their eyes met. "You've been very thoughtful," she added softly.

He deflected her appreciation in a western drawl. "Aw, shucks, ma'am. 'Tweren't nothin'."

She raised herself off the pillows she'd stacked together to slip on the robe. A cramp in her shoulder sent a shooting pain through the back of her head, and she winced briefly.

Discomfort crossed Chad's features, too. Was that a sympathy wince?

"Does it hurt very much?" he asked.

"I can live with the agony of waiting to buy my own diamonds."

"That might be sooner than you think."

"It's nice to know you believe in the business abilities of a total stranger."

"Not total." He shifted in the chair, ill at ease. "What I meant was, does your head hurt very much?"

"I've had worse headaches during tax season."

"Haven't we all," he replied with a chuckle.

When she started to shrug into the robe, he quickly got up to assist her, holding the silky garment for her arms, then gliding it over her shoulders, his fingertips gently brushing her neck. Fluttering sensations danced along her nerve endings.

Pay the piper for that particular dance or end it, she decided.

"I can't say I don't have a free moment now to listen to your business proposition," she said.

For the first time, his eyes skittered away from hers. "Not here. Not until you're completely well."

She started to protest. But, she realized with some amazement, she was drawing enormous pleasure from Chad's visit despite having always considered herself quite independent and solitary. Maybe it was because she was somewhat incapacitated and didn't know anyone else in the area, but she couldn't bring herself to chase him away by insisting that his business be stated and possibly dealt with immediately. Presumably, that was their primary reason for staying in contact.

But she decided to have a closer look at his business card as soon as he left. Then she remembered that it was in her purse, back on Sunrise Key.

Chad was angling the conversation away from business and on to current news topics.

In the next couple of hours, they discovered they had many attitudes and interests in common. She suggested that he go home and get some sleep, but he remained until the doctor made his evening rounds.

It was determined that Denyse should stay in the hospital a couple of days longer. If she returned to Sunrise Key any sooner, it could be difficult to get her back to the hospital promptly if she took an unexpected turn for the worse. Also, she recalled suffering from a mild seasickness during her other boat trips, and didn't want to risk that now.

She tried not to wrestle with the thoughts drifting through her consciousness — a remembered scream, a wet floor in the warehouse, a party for a "birthday" she was growing increasingly suspicious of. Was she simply taking the easy way out by remaining in the hospital for a couple of extra days?

She'd allow herself that, she decided.

Soon, Chad could hardly stay awake, having scarcely dozed in a chair in the waiting room the night before. And Denyse couldn't stay awake, despite having slept through most of that same period.

"Would you leave me another business card with your phone numbers?" she asked as he rose to leave.

He patted the pockets of his beige slacks and brown shirt. "I don't seem to have any with me. But I'll write down the numbers." He jotted them on a pad on her nightstand.

That wouldn't give her any direct clues about his business. She wished she'd paid closer attention to his card when he gave it to her, but it had been dark outside, and then Wick had distracted her.

"Call me if you need anything, anything at all," Chad said in parting.

Drowsily, she noted that he didn't promise another visit.

Chapter 4

Denyse had a roommate as of the next morning, a rather snobbish woman around forty, hospitalized for some routine tests. She seemed more the type for a private than a semi-private room, but perhaps her bank account hadn't kept pace with her airs.

Denyse was glad to have the bed nearest the window, although it would soon be too dark to see anything. She read the latest financial magazines, brought by a volunteer, while the woman visited with a couple of friends on the opposite side of the ceilings-to-floor drape that separated their beds. Denyse had tuned out their conversation hours ago.

She was unaware when a new voice was added.

One of her roommate's visitors called out loudly, "Hey, there's a guy here to see you. Okay to send him on back?"

Who's behind the curtain? Bachelor Number One, Bachelor Number Two, or Bachelor Number Three?

Technically, for her, Bachelor Number One had been Bob Farrell, an attorney in Boston. Their living-together arrangements hadn't survived the tax season, but they remained friends.

So, would Chad and Wick be her prize for today? Perhaps she wouldn't see Chad again until she returned to Sunrise Key and was open for business.

All day, she'd been prepared for a visit, hoping to see Chad more than she wanted to admit. She was wearing the sunshine-colored robe with lipstick and freshly brushed hair.

An arrangement of brightly colored flowers appeared around the curtain.

Maybe this was just a deliveryman.

But the deliverer and the sender were one and the same. Chad.

She fully realized in that moment that it would always be Chad who could be depended upon. Chad would be there for anyone to whom he had committed himself.

She recognized also in that moment that Wick had been nothing more than an occasional brief flicker in her thoughts for the past twenty-four hours. It was Chad whose visit she'd been awaiting, and there was no point in kidding herself that her eagerness for more time with him didn't exist.

Wick cut a romantic figure. But he couldn't cut it with Denyse Benton, if he was even interested. Her feet were rooted too deeply in terra firma for her to be swept off of them by the next high tide.

She could understand how her mother had fallen in love with her father, if Wick were as much like her father as Wick implied. But, while her mother's and father's dreams may have melded, the reality of their backgrounds and lifestyles had been too different for either to make enough adjustments to be truly happy. Denyse had more sense of self and was several years older than her mother had been when she'd married Dennis Benton.

Denyse's conversation with Chad was comfortable that evening, but still general. He obviously intended neither to discuss business nor share detailed personal information.

At least this time, he made a date for the future, if offering to rent a VCR and some movies for her hospital viewing pleasure constituted a date.

It was *High Noon* at sunset.

Chad's selecting two of her all-time, most adored movies hadn't been entirely luck. They had discovered similar interests in movies, literature, and music before today.

He'd been able to arrive at the hospital in

the late afternoon, and they'd already watched *Charade.*

Denyse's eyes often wandered from the movie — despite its status on her personal Top Ten list — in the direction of the bouquet of two-dozen yellow roses that Chad had brought, along with the movies and a huge bag of popcorn. Her thoughts were wandering, too, down a freshly paved memory lane.

"Yellow roses are my favorites," she'd exclaimed in delight — like a girl receiving her first prom corsage, she'd chided herself later. Remembering that they matched her new robe, she'd asked, "How did you know that yellow is my favorite color?"

"Maybe I just associate you with sunshine, or at least with sunrise."

"Because of Sunrise Key." A tinge of disappointment crept into her voice.

"No," he'd responded softly. "More because those dawn-gray eyes of yours remind me of the promise of a new day, close to sunrise." He added swiftly, with an endearing touch of shyness, "Or because you're bright and warm, like the morning's glow."

"Nobody's ever accused me of being warm before," was the comment she'd almost flipped back at him. But she restrained herself, recognizing that she often relied on humor to distance herself from potential suitors.

Suitor. What a funny, old-fashioned word. But it seemed to fit the gentlemanly Chad, even in this Gulf Coast location too far south to be considered part of the Deep South.

She already knew this was one man she didn't intend to discourage, by suitor or any other term.

In fact, he was sharing her bed right now, his lanky legs protruding several inches beyond her own. Her roommate's visitors had appropriated all the chairs before Chad's arrival, so naturally Denyse had invited him to sit on the bed.

And just as naturally, he was soon propped on the pillows alongside her, his legs stretched out in front of him. Those legs were clad in pale green slacks, and he wore a contrasting forest green shirt.

When their thighs accidentally touched on the narrow bed, neither moved away. And somehow, the side of his left thigh was now lightly pressed along the full length of her right. His arm was draped loosely around her shoulders.

While Gary Cooper and Grace Kelly shot bad guys, Denyse fought her own battle with regard to what appeared to be a very good guy.

Right person, she'd begun to believe. But certainly the wrong place.

If it weren't for the hospital setting, complete with a roommate and her two visitors, one sheet of fabric away, Denyse might have been tempted to forsake *High Noon* and invite Chad to collaborate on a "do-it-ourselves" script. She wondered if Chad was better able to concentrate on the movie than she was.

Does Blue Cross pay if you have fun in the hospital? she mused.

That didn't sound at all like the person who'd left Boston a few days ago, Denyse realized. Amazing, and more than a little disquieting, what a bump on the head could do.

The doctor arrived within minutes of Gary Cooper grinding his sheriff's badge into the dust.

"We usually discharge people in the morning, but I see no reason why you can't go home tonight if you want to," Dr. Fornier said.

Back to the unexplained scream, the swamp, and the financial problems. Back where Chad had no reason to visit daily. Thanks a lot, Doc, Denyse thought. Aloud, she said, "Sure. I might as well."

"I'll drive you," Chad volunteered. "We can drive to the far end of Captiva where I have a condo, and take my boat from there so you won't have to spend so much ocean-going time."

Denyse didn't argue with that.

She wasn't looking forward to putting on the same dirty jeans and T-shirt that she wore for her swamp tromp, but she had no choice. "I guess you'd better wait outside so I can dress," Denyse said as soon as Dr. Fornier made his exit.

"Don't dress until I've been outside," Chad replied, in a reversal of her statement.

"You brought something for me to wear?"

"It's not a mink coat, I promise. So don't turn it down in advance. I left it in the trunk of the car for whenever you were discharged."

So he'd been expecting to escort her home, although they'd never discussed it. How had he known that Wick wouldn't turn up and be her choice of escort?

Chad came back several minutes later, carrying a large box with glittery wrapping and bow. "There's a choice of two outfits in there," he told her in advance. "For one, I had to guess at your size. In case I was wrong, the other is one-size-fits-all. I figured you'd like to put on something fresh, and I still haven't had time to pick up any of your things from Sunrise Key."

She removed the wrappings and read the name on the box. "Dressed for Excess."

"It's a new boutique in Fort Myers."

She gave him an amused smile, framed by lifted eyebrows.

"I had to be there anyway," he said quickly, returning her grin.

For what? she wanted to ask. Buying clothes for other women? But he avoided discussing personal details, so she didn't pursue it.

"Let's see how good you are at sizing up women," she said in a tone more teasing than she felt.

He disappeared on the other side of the room-dividing curtain, quipping, "This reminds me of *It Happened One Night*."

The ladies on the opposite side of the curtain welcomed him with the same enthusiasm that Claudette Colbert had felt for Clark Gable, Denyse noted.

Opening the box, she found a swirling, full, tiered red skirt like the type she associated with pirate movies, only in a shorter, modern length. Beneath it was a white peasant blouse with a large, lace-edged ruffle embellishing the scooped neck.

The skirt fit as long as she made a choice between fastening the waistband button or breathing. She certainly wouldn't point out to Chad that her waistline wasn't as small as he'd thought.

But there wasn't much she could do about the size of the blouse. Dressed for Excess might mean excess material as far as that was concerned. A significant surplus of fabric dangled about the breasts she'd previously thought adequate. She'd avoid making it obvious to Chad that she didn't completely fit his concept of the ideal woman.

She pulled out the next garment with some trepidation. It was a long, abstractly multi-colored strip of fabric, accompanied by a booklet explaining the style as a *pareo* from Tahiti, with instructions for tying it in different fashions, ranging from not-too-subtly seductive to very seductive. And she didn't even have a bra, since she hadn't been wearing one for her walk in the swamp.

Suddenly bashful that her figure might not be entirely up to Chad's expectations, she managed a semi-modest wrap-and-tie style that left one shoulder bare and showed a flash of her left thigh through the overlap of the fabric whenever she took a step.

She pulled the room drape halfway open.

Chad looked up from his chatting. She'd like to think that if eyes could gasp, his did at that moment.

"Wow," was all he said. After a pause, he added, "I confess to hoping that you'd pick that outfit."

"I didn't have much choice." She couldn't hold back the laughter. "I'm afraid the other one represented a lot of wishful thinking on your part, well beyond hope."

"What do you mean?" he asked innocently.

"The blouse is a little large." She chuckled again. "A lot large."

He scrutinized her bosom, his eyes lingering in a visual caress. She felt a flush she hadn't felt since she was about seventeen. And worse, she sensed the buds of her breasts blossoming, hardening, wanting the touch of more than his gaze, searing as that was.

He looked up sheepishly, his eyes meeting hers, his lingering gaze continuing in a different manner.

"Sorry," he said. "I guessed at size thirty-four."

"Thirty-four is right," she blurted out. Then, still embarrassed, she turned back to the bed, picked up the blouse, and checked the label. "This is size forty-four. The salesclerk must have misunderstood." Or Chad's a good liar, Denyse added to herself. But she suspected that he was sufficiently experienced with women not to be that far wrong.

"I can exchange it for you," he offered. "Unless you don't like it."

"I like it fine." Oddly and unbeknownst to him, the outfit had become Chad's means of associating himself in her mind with *The Crimson Pirate* starring Burt Lancaster, a role she'd previously associated with Wick. Chad was doing quite a thorough job of obsessing her thoughts.

She still was trying not to face the possible truth about either or both of them. She attributed that to waiting until all the evidence was accumulated — one reason she continued to await personal and business revelations from Chad rather than asking the usual, obvious questions.

"I like the outfit very much." And, to paraphrase Wick, there hasn't been enough swashbuckling in my life, she thought. "I might as well return the blouse myself so I can try on the replacement." And exchange the skirt at the same time, she added in her mind, determined not to bring up the fact that her waistline wasn't as small as mentally pictured by Chad. She doubted that the salesclerk had made two mistakes in providing the requested sizes.

They gathered up her few belongings and walked to the parking lot.

Maybe he could have afforded the mink coat and the diamonds, Denyse realized, when they arrived at his car, a sleek red Jaguar.

"I'd offer to take you to dinner," Chad said as they drove away, "but it's probably better to get you to bed right away." With a sideways glance and a grin, he added, "To rest, I mean."

"What I'd rather have more than anything," she sighed wistfully, "is a hamburger and a milkshake. How do prisoners and expatriates survive?"

"You've only been in unsolitary confinement for three days," he reminded her with a laugh. Nonetheless, he honored her request with a stop at the nearest hamburger emporium.

"I don't think I'm dressed to go in," she realized aloud.

"You look fine to me. But if you want to eat in the car, I don't mind having you all to myself."

When Chad returned with the order, he proposed a toast, holding aloft his paper cup. *"Salud, pesetas, y amor."*

"Translation, please. I want to know what I'm drinking to."

"Heath, wealth, and love."

She eagerly took a sip of chocolate milkshake. Reveling in each other's company, they savored the burgers and shakes as if dinner were prime rib and champagne.

As they drove across the bridge linking the island of Sanibel with the Gulf Coast of the Florida peninsula, Denyse said, "I almost forgot." For a little while in Chad's company, she had forgotten. "Before I fell, I heard an incredible scream." She frowned, as if wrinkling her brow could aid her. "I don't think the cry came from the direction of the building, though."

"Was it a weird sort of wail that reached across the swamp and wrung out the depths of your soul?"

"That's a pretty close description." She took a deep breath before asking, "How did you know?"

"It was probably a limpkin. That's a long-billed, long-legged wading bird with a jerky gait. A limpkin can be hilarious to watch, but the sound it makes occasionally —" Chad gave a mock shudder. "It's like a feathered version of comedy and tragedy."

"The noise didn't exactly sound human,

now that I think about it. But it sure startled me."

"Wait until you hear the roar of an alligator. You'll swear that a lion has settled on Sunrise Key."

"Tell me about the other wildlife there. I saw beautiful birds in the preserve."

She described some of the species she'd watched, and Chad tentatively identified them. The pink ones with the flat, paddlelike bills were called roseate spoonbills. Large white birds could be herons or egrets. The smaller species the color of a robin's egg might be the little blue heron. The long-necked bird that spread its dark wings like a feathered version of Dracula, to dry them after diving for fish, was an anhinga or snakebird. Another might have been a hawk circling high against the sky. Even she had recognized the pelicans and gulls.

The drive was requiring longer than she had anticipated, around an hour since the route traveled south some distance before connecting with the road that doubled back north as well as west to the far end of Captiva.

Before they reached the short bridge between Sanibel and Captiva, the headlights caught a pair of bright little orbs immediately ahead.

"Oooh," Denyse couldn't help crying out.

Chad swerved the car away just in time, braking abruptly at the side of the highway.

"Are you all right?" he asked anxiously.

"Yes," she replied, rather puzzled. "Aren't you?"

"Of course. But I was afraid I'd jarred you too much or something. Your head isn't worse?"

"I'm fine, really," she assured him, and a warmth at his concern suddenly surrounded her. "What was that thing?"

"I'll find out." When Chad reached over to get a flashlight from the glove compartment, his arm brushed against her bare thigh.

They both drew in a quick breath at that moment. Then he opened the door.

"Wait here," he said.

But Denyse was already halfway out the door. She was an ardent animal lover, although she hadn't had much opportunity to put it into practice.

They hurried back along the road. A baby raccoon started to scurry away at the beam of the flashlight. Then, confused and bewildered, it decided to remain by its mother, who had been hit by an earlier car.

"We can't do much for the mother,"

Chad said, "but I don't like to leave any creature suffering." He hunkered down for a closer examination. "She's already dead."

Denyse reached to pick up the baby.

"Don't do that," Chad snapped.

She bristled. "Why not?"

"He might bite you. He might even have rabies. I'll try to herd him away from the highway."

"He's too little to survive by himself."

Chad's frustration with their lack of alternatives was obvious in his irascible tone. "Well, that's life."

"And death." The words flared out of her. Then she hesitated. The little raccoon was more frightened and skittish than vicious. But she wasn't eager to risk rabies. "I'll figure out a way," she mumbled, more to herself than to Chad.

"If you're so determined, let me do it," he said, with mildly disgusted resignation.

"Why? Are you immune to rabies? You're the one who wanted to leave him to die," she argued.

"No, I didn't. Damn it, Denyse, we're hitting on one of my major philosophical conflicts."

"Well, what did Aristotle and Plato have to say about raccoons?" Her question dripped with sarcasm.

"I mean, how much should one interfere with the natural order of things? Especially if the interference presents the victims with a new set of problems without having solved the source of the original problems."

"That sounds mentally agonizing and all," Denyse said with a remaining vestige of sarcasm, "but I don't understand what you're talking about. It doesn't sound like it has much to do with an orphaned baby raccoon."

"Oh, hell, I guess I wasn't cut out to be a great philosopher. But in order for this particular raccoon to survive now, you'll have to feed him by hand. Then you'll always have to feed him. He'll never be able to be free because he won't have developed the necessary survival skills."

"But at least he'll live."

Chad tucked the flashlight under his arm and proceeded to unbutton his shirt.

Her thoughts were temporarily distracted from the raccoon. Was Chad's chest smooth, or did a masculine mat of hair flourish there? she found herself wondering. She managed to ask, "What are you doing?"

"Giving you the shirt off my back, at least indirectly."

She fought an urge to reach out and assist him. Soon his muscular chest was revealed, with a scattering of dark hairs. Not too little. Not too much. Just right, Denyse decided.

She only peripherally realized that she was giving him the same prolonged scrutiny that he had lavished on that general, but clothed, area of her body earlier in the evening.

Chad wrapped the dark green fabric of his shirt sleeves around his hands as protection, then scooped up the frightened baby raccoon in the remaining fabric.

By the time they drove away, the raccoon was curled in a sort of protective nest of green fabric atop Denyse's lap, at her insistence. Chad's yellow roses were banished from her lap to the center of the seat, coming between them incongruently.

In her condominium in Boston, she couldn't have a pet — not a dog or cat, certainly not an adorable little raccoon. Denyse had achingly missed having a pet when she was a child, since her mother and stepfather had occupied a city apartment similar to the one Denyse now owned. In her adult years, she'd simply shoved the pet prospect to the back of her mind as unfeasible. Now she was feeling immense pleasure from the warm, furry creature cuddled against her.

Perhaps now was the time for reassessment. For acknowledging longings for other things she may have missed.

Her father's bequest was forcing her to make new decisions. Those decisions might include some new directions, both professional and personal.

Although fully career-oriented, Denyse had declined offers of excellent positions with her employer's clients in order to maximize the scope of her experience. Through the accounting firm, she had gained exposure to various types of business operations. She'd been planning to start her own financial consulting and accounting firm in a few years. Instead, she'd suddenly found herself the keeper of an inn that was no longer in. Although she'd tried to focus first on developing a comprehensive management analysis, the ultimate choices had remained paramount in her mind.

She might try to retain Sunrise Key, and attempt to develop Sunriseset into a successful resort once again. But she probably wouldn't have that opportunity since the inheritance tax would be due soon.

She could attempt to peddle her legacy. Even with the rising interest rates and ailing economy, a buyer might be found for Sunrise Key. Although taxes would voraciously devour the majority of the selling price, the remaining small percentage would more than enable her to live comfortably for the rest of her life.

Yuck. Live comfortably for the rest of her life. Why did that sound awful?

Probably because she didn't like the prospect that life would be already fixed in place. She couldn't imagine life without some sort of daily challenge beyond who would win a tennis match at the country club. Being a lady of leisure for the balance of her sojourn on earth sounded stifling.

For now, her primary goal was reestablishing the comfortable rapport she'd felt with Chad before their raccoon rescue.

She asked him about a store they were passing.

Soon the tension that had come between them lifted and they once again fell into easy conversation.

By the time they reached Chad's condominium, they'd decided to name the raccoon Clayton, after Clayton Moore, who'd played the role of the Lone Ranger, because of the similar black mask around his eyes.

"Let me carry Clayton," Chad said as he stopped the car at the dock where his cabin cruiser was tied up.

He came around the Jaguar and opened

the passenger door, gently scooping Clayton off Denyse's lap. A delicious tremor echoed through her as the backs of his hands caressed her thighs, lingering longer than necessary. There was a hitch in his voice as he said, "I'd invite the two of you up to the condo, but due to some repainting —"

Just then, Clayton wriggled in his hands, considering escape for the first time. "Whoa, little fella," Chad admonished with such tenderness that Denyse realized it was unlikely that he would have left Clayton to fend for himself even if she hadn't been there.

The cabin cruiser rapidly bridged the distance between Captiva and Sunrise Key before Denyse really had time to develop her fantasy of the bare-chested Chad as a pirate captain spiriting her away toward the Spanish Main. She scarcely registered an impression of the attractiveness of the cabin cruiser with its polished light wood and gleaming brass fixtures.

An hour later, they were in the resort's kitchen, laughing while they tried to concoct a formula acceptable to a baby raccoon — adding this, starting fresh, subtracting that. Finally, Clayton deigned to accept one of their recipes and began sucking from the finger of a rubber glove with a hole punched through it.

"I don't know whether to put this shirt back on or not," Chad had said jokingly after they'd arrived. "I might get fleas or something."

I might have to flee if you don't, Denyse thought. Or else wriggle around here as if I had fleas myself.

The shirt remained off. So did her hormonal balance.

Watching Denyse hold Clayton in her arms and feed him, Chad remarked, "You'd make a good mother."

"That isn't on my list of things to do," Denyse replied, wondering why she was, in a way, seizing this opportunity to inform Chad of her interests and goals. Surely, it was too early in this relationship to be discussing whether or not to have children, she told herself. Yet, somehow, she wanted him to know. She didn't want to be disappointed if they progressed further, then found their lifestyles wouldn't mesh.

It's ridiculous to be thinking of that after only a few days, Denyse chided herself. But the fact was, she was afraid of falling in love with someone who couldn't love her back, exactly as she was. At this point in her life, she couldn't imagine "having it all" while also maintaining some level of sanity.

"I think Clayton is as far as my parental instincts extend right now," she added for emphasis.

"I think my present instincts are inclined toward building cages," Chad said. "Let me see what I can rustle up in the way of a home for Clayton."

Carlos came into the kitchen just then, overhearing Chad's last remark. "The other side of your duplex is cleaned up if someone needs a place to stay, Señorita Benton," he pointed out helpfully.

"That might be a bit lavish," Chad replied.

"Carlos, meet Clayton." Denyse turned to introduce the two.

Soon, Chad and Carlos had fashioned a makeshift raccoon condo from some chicken wire found in the supply building. Jacques came to get a snack, and joined in the project.

The pen adjoined the kitchen, beneath trees that shaded the area during the day. Clayton happily settled in and soon went to sleep.

"Did you hear him say, 'Goodnight, *kemo sabes*'?" Chad asked.

"No, because that would be the wrong line," she replied with a laugh. "If he's the

Lone Ranger, we're the Tontos. Lone Ranger there," she gestured teasingly, "Tontos here."

The sound of shattering glass disturbed the quiet night. They turned to see that Jacques had dropped his glass of milk on the concrete paving outside the kitchen. Even in the moonlight, the terror on his face was evident. *"Tonton?"* he muttered anxiously, with the lilt of Caribbean French. "Here?"

Chad hastened to give him a reassuring pat on the shoulder and explain in a murmur so low Denyse could barely hear, "No *tonton*. We were kidding around about old movie characters." He clarified how Clayton had been named.

Jacques relaxed and grinned, returning to the kitchen for a new glass of milk.

Chad suppressed a yawn, checked his watch, and glanced back in the direction of the blissfully slumbering raccoon. "I'm tempted to crawl in there with him and save myself a trip back home tonight."

"But it's only a few minutes across the water to your condo on Captiva."

"No, I'm staying at my house in Fort Myers. Didn't I mention the repainting —"

"You don't have to drive back tonight if you don't want to," Denyse blurted out. "I mean, Carlos said the other side of my duplex is cleaned up and available."

"If you're sure you don't mind."

I'll mind having you so close but not with me, she thought. Suddenly, the intensity of her desires dismayed her. She picked up her belongings, and they began the stroll along the shell-strewn path to her duplex.

Chapter 5

Chad started to offer his arm to her for support, then decided against it, stuffing both hands into his pockets.

Her duplex came into view, soft moonlight bathing the modest structure in a palatial hue of white silver. That same moonglow burnished Chad's bare flesh, and Denysc's gaze was involuntarily drawn to him. As a result, she wasn't watching where she was going and her sandal caught on the edge of a large shell, causing her to stumble.

Chad's hands shot out of his pockets. He caught her and wrapped her protectively in his arms, offering her the strength of his body for support.

Never was she in more danger of falling and hurting herself, she realized as she reveled in the dizzying sensations of Chad's body against hers. At last she could press against and touch that chest that felt even warmer than she expected, as if from the caress of the moonlight.

"You shouldn't have left the hospital yet," Chad was saying, concern evident in his tone. "I'm going to take you back there right now."

"Chad, I tripped on a shell. I'm all right, really," she said with a sigh of content and desire.

"You're sure," he asked softly in her ear.

"Positive."

Still, neither of them made a move. She didn't know how many moments trickled past while she remained securely locked in his embrace and their breaths quickened together.

"This path is pretty treacherous," he mumbled finally, stepping back as he released her, leaving her bereft.

Then, to her amazement, he suddenly lifted her up off the ground and into his arms.

"Chad!" she exclaimed, then stifled her protest in favor of snuggling against him and slipping her arms around his neck.

Much as it sullied her ego, she realized his rapid breathing wasn't entirely for the same reason as hers. At five-feet eight-inches, she wasn't exactly a featherweight.

"Chad, put me down," she said without much fervor. "I can walk. Really. I'm too heavy to carry."

"You're just right," he puffed. Teasingly, he managed to add, "Woman, do not interfere with my macho display of strength." She was too overwhelmed by the feel of his body against hers to protest any further.

"Just be glad you have a straight path and not a skyscraper like King Kong, or even that huge staircase in *Gone With the Wind*," she joked back.

"But, oh lady, what went on at the top of those stairs."

Denyse closed her eyes, reveling in the sensations washing over her. The sensuous flex of his muscles through the thin fabric of the pareo set her entire body on fire.

Chad shifted her slightly to reach for the doorknob, and a heady feeling of warmth spiralled through her as her scarcely clothed breast pressed against his chest.

"It's locked," he observed with some consternation. "Nobody locks doors here."

"Proper Bostonians do." Except she didn't feel at all like a proper Bostonian. "Old habits are hard to break." Reluctantly, she removed her arm from around his neck where it had anchored her to him. "The key is in my jeans pocket, you'll have to put me down," she said with a trace of sadness.

Gently, he eased her toward a standing position and desire streaked through her as her thigh encountered the proof that his passion had grown as great as her own. He continued to keep one arm around her for support while she fished for the key with trembling fingers.

He took the key from her, opening the door. "Maybe you're right. I certainly wouldn't want anything to happen to you. I'll switch on the lights, turn down the bed, make sure you're settled in." He then added, as much with remorse as with gentlemanly promise, "I'll come in only for a minute."

Cool air beckoned from within. Consuela or Carlos must have turned on the air conditioner earlier. It occurred to Denyse that Wick might be ensconced inside again, and she silently prayed he wasn't.

Through the open door, moonlight illumined a narrow path leading straight to the bed. Chad guided her forward along this moonlit path, still offering his arm for support but otherwise holding his tensed body as far from hers as possible.

"Let me take your shoes off so you don't have to bend down and get dizzy," he said.

With unaccustomed obedience, she sat on the edge of the bed and held out one foot.

Dizzy might have been preferable to the chaotic sensations coursing through her as Chad knelt and slowly unbuckled her sandal, his hands stroking the arch of her foot.

If Prince Charming had been taking off a

sandal instead of putting on a glass slipper, he and Cinderella might never have made it back to the palace in time for the wedding, Denyse thought distractedly.

He repeated the same procedure with her other foot, only this time one hand cradled her ankle, then slipped an inch higher before he suddenly withdrew.

"I guess you can take it from here," he murmured in a subdued tone.

"Uh-huh," she managed to answer from deep within her throat.

Their gazes locked together and, as he rose from the floor, she found herself standing, too, matching the length of her body to his. She was uncertain which sensations were reverberating from within her and which were coming from Chad.

Eventually, Chad said softly, "I'm afraid to ask for a good-night kiss."

"What makes you think I'd say no?" Denyse murmured back, surprised at her forthright manner.

"I'm afraid if you say yes, I might not be able to stop with one kiss."

She turned her lips toward his, offering an unspoken invitation, trembling in the need to feel his mouth on hers.

Chad's lips brushed hers gently, then returned for a series of tender, searching, tantalizing kisses. His tongue guided hers in a dance of desire.

Then Chad abruptly abandoned her mouth, leaving it empty and longing. He pulled back and said huskily, "I warned you I wouldn't want to stop with one kiss."

After a heartbeat's hesitation, Denyse replied softly. "I don't recall asking you to stop." She crossed the invisible line between them, her lips seeking his as though magnetized.

With that same magnetism, their bodies pressed together at last. Denyse reveled in the feel of his broad chest against her.

Chad's embrace became a symphony of caresses coaxing wondrous notes from her body. Slowly, sensuously, he molded her to him, drawing back ever so slightly once to ask an unspoken question with his eyes, and finding the answer in her own moon-gilded ones.

The shoulder knot securing her pareo proved no challenge for Chad, and the garment drifted to the floor. He held her eager body still tighter against his own, and the peaks of her breasts responded willingly to the firmness of his chest with its mat of hair.

She was glad there were minimal barriers between them now. But uncertainty suddenly crept in. Maybe she should focus on something to keep her on her guard. On something. On anything. Casual liaisons had never been her style. At the risk of sounding too prim and old-fashioned even to herself, she had to wonder how she'd feel the morning after. And all the mornings after that. She barely knew Chad — yet here she was thrilling at getting to know him better . . .

Get control of yourself, she told herself. At least make this a rational decision. Think of something else for a few minutes to ward off this spell he's casting on you.

Too late. She gave up hope of retaining her sensibilities as Chad's trousers found their way to the floor.

She was trapped in a whirlwind of passion. Her desire churned and thickened with Chad's every kiss and caress, her every move orchestrated by the man controlling this whirlpool of sensation.

She realized without a doubt that she had no wish to escape this now, no matter what tomorrow might bring.

Chad's fingertips traced beneath the band of her lace panties, then he pulled his hands away. Denyse moaned at her loss.

But those hands responded to new demands, gliding up to cradle her warm, aching breasts. His fingers fanned out, one by one brushing over the sensitized tips as his mouth murmured against hers, "Denyse, Denyse . . ."

His thumbs flicked back and forth across her nipples as his lips tantalized her earlobe and he darted his tongue into the tingling hollow of her ear.

It seemed he didn't have enough hands as every millimeter of her body simultaneously clamored for his touch. Yet, with the two he did have, he succeeded quite effortlessly in making her a willing captive of their passion.

His burning mouth trailed kisses along the side of her neck, then quivered against the pounding pulse in her throat as she tilted back her head in abandon. Her hands alternately caressed and clenched the muscles of his back.

At last his kisses meandered downward into the valley between her breasts. Then his tongue wandered and, slowly circling one summit, his moist lips staked their claim. She gasped with pleasure.

She slid her hand beneath the fabric that still separated them, her fingers trembling against the warm, supple flesh of his abdomen. There was a sharp intake of his breath as her palm slipped lower, intent on freeing the full power of his manhood. He cupped her buttocks in his grasp, and they lowered themselves onto the bed.

At last, her fingers enveloped the proof of his desire as he murmured her name. A quiver began beneath his caresses, along her thighs, then moving along the inside of her legs, journeying toward her warm core.

With expert kisses Chad guided her head back toward the waiting pillow.

The pillow connected with her head at the still-tender spots where she'd fallen and she was unable to suppress a tiny outcry at the unexpected pain.

Chad yanked his head back in surprise, and through the cloud of desire, determined the reason for her exclamation.

A look of concern crossed his face as he ran his fingertips through her auburn hair, gingerly avoiding the tender spot.

"I'm all right. Really," she assured him softly, having twisted her head into a comfortable position.

Yet Chad pulled slowly away from her, first ceasing his exploration of her thigh, then withdrawing with one last, long caress. He unlaced his fingertips from her hair. He struggled to regulate his breathing, to exert control over himself.

Denyse felt suspended, almost as though she was levitating upward, yearning toward his touch. Thrills raced through her when at last he again inclined his head toward hers.

But instead of kissing her waiting mouth, his lips gently brushed her cheek in a manner unworthy of even a brotherly peck.

He murmured, "Not tonight, dear. You have a headache."

"Chad." His name escaped her in an agony of longing. "I'm okay."

Still, he moved away from her quickly, off the bed, grabbing his trousers. Well, if he didn't want her any more than that, she wasn't about to beg.

Yet while making his exit, he backed away, as though unwilling to tear his eyes from her until the final moment. "I'll be next door," he reminded her unnecessarily. "Just knock on the wall if you need anything."

Then he was gone, closing the door behind him and leaving Denyse alone in the dark, in a mood blacker than the night surrounding her. Any pleasure she might have felt at his consideration was severely tempered by her dejection that maybe he didn't really want her anyway. The room suddenly felt like an incredibly empty void.

Knock on the wall.
The hours ticked past. Denyse remained

ticked off — mostly at herself.

Knock on the wall if you need anything.

She definitely needed something. Chad. But she most certainly would never tap out an S.O.S. on the wall for him.

She needed Chad. How did a reasonably healthy, but usually restrained Certified Public Accountant from Boston explain that? She couldn't justify it to herself, much less explain it to him or anyone else.

She'd met him less than a week ago. It wasn't possible to fall in love with someone in such a brief period.

Love, ha! Of course, it couldn't be love. Admit it, Denyse. It's pure lust, even if it is an extra powerful sexual attraction like you've never felt before.

Maybe not, reasoned another voice within her. She'd sensed some sort of special rapport with Chad, even on that first evening.

No wonder her mild headache had returned. All this arguing back and forth in her brain was enough to cause that. And her emotions were muscling in too, tugging in very opposite directions.

She'd never heard of a bump on the head acting as an aphrodisiac. Perhaps she'd discovered some unknown acupressure point. If so, she could establish acupressure aphrodisiac clinics across the country, she thought, trying to cheer herself up.

She tried to focus on the dull ache at the back of her head, hoping it would overwhelm her so that she could forget the different sort of ache assailing the rest of her body. Every nerve ending seemed to be a sensitive antenna, seeking, awaiting the return of Chad's strong form against hers.

Knock on the wall if you need anything.

She tried to rationalize. Maybe it was a side effect of some medication they'd given her at the hospital. More likely a side effect of all the events of the past week, with her once-secure life abruptly uprooted and the golden dream of sudden good fortune tarnished by recent circumstance and problems.

Perhaps it was just a basic physical need. She was a sensual, modern woman and there had been no man in her life since her relationship with Bob Farrell had been mutually and cordially terminated. Even the parting with Bob had lacked any special flair, she realized, comparing her feelings then to the ones Chad had ignited within her.

Strange how this basic need had surfaced only now. Had grown rampantly, demandingly only a few days after meeting Chad.

She trembled with the recollection of his flesh against hers.

Knock on the wall.

It would be so simple, so easy. Should it be one gentle tap? Or a more assertive trio? Or a longer *bom-bom-bede-bom-bom-BOM-BOM!*

Stop this foolishness, she commanded herself. Of course she wasn't going anywhere near the wall. She had too much self-respect for that. After all, Chad had left her of his own accord. Left her feeling more empty and alone than she'd known possible.

She rolled angrily onto her other side, staring toward the bathroom door rather than the partition that separated the cottages.

Several minutes later, she clambered out of bed in annoyance. Maybe if she weren't lying supine on the bed he'd so nearly shared with her, she could stop remembering, could extinguish this desire blazing through her body.

Besides, since she couldn't sleep, she might as well read a book or a magazine or something. Crossing the dark and unfamiliar room toward the light switch, she stumbled against the straight-backed chair, banging it into the desk. Irascibly, Denyse continued toward the cottage entrance, searching for the main light switch.

She gasped, startled, as the front door burst open. Then she drew in her breath again at the sight greeting her.

Chad was a tall silhouette against the silvery moonlight, outlines of his muscular chest and arms visible. He had pulled on his slacks in haste. She was attired as he'd left her — bare but for lacy panties.

"What is it?" he asked anxiously. "What do you need?"

"I, uh . . ." She was ridiculously incoherent. "Uh, nothing."

"But you knocked on the wall."

She'd forgotten the racket of the errant chair, thinking for one brief ecstatic moment that he'd come back to her entirely of his own volition, that his passion must be as demanding as her own. She took pleasure in realizing, however, that he must have been lying awake, too, to have responded so quickly to the supposed signal.

"I'm sorry," she stammered, acutely embarrassed by her near nudity. "I accidentally tipped over the chair when I got up to find something to read." She emphasized with stubborn pride, "I didn't knock on the wall."

"Then I'm the one who should apologize, for busting in on you like this." His eyes were wandering over the peaks of her breasts, down the curved slope to her waist, along her stomach, unable to meet her eyes despite the sincere tone of his words. With effort, he pulled his gaze back to her face, where it belonged. "Well, since I'm here anyway, why don't you get back in bed and I'll get you whatever you want."

Denyse stifled the tempting response and complied instead. She welcomed the sanctuary of the cool sheets, inserting herself between them until the top one covered her shoulder. She turned on her side to watch him.

Only then did Chad switch on the desk lamp. He scanned the bookshelves above the desk. "What do you want?"

"I don't care. Anything," she lied. "I was just going to read for a while since I couldn't get to sleep."

"Is the pain bad?" Chad's eyes reflected the concern in his voice. "Didn't the hospital give you any pills?"

"My head hardly hurts at all, so I haven't taken any more of the medicine. I just couldn't get to sleep —" She interrupted herself to add hurriedly, "I napped all day, you know."

"The doctor probably intended for you to sleep tonight, too. The medicine probably contains a sedative. Where is it?"

"You would have made a great head nurse," Denyse teased, inwardly glowing at his concern. "The brown bottle on the bathroom shelf."

She admired his strong back, trimming at the waist, as he crossed the room.

He returned with a pill and a glass of water, standing over her as if she were a child, while she swallowed it.

He selected a thin volume from the bookshelf and sat down gingerly at the far edge of the bed.

Torture. Agony.

How could he do this to her? It was cruel for him to place himself within her reach when he didn't want her to touch him.

"Suppose I read you a story," he joked, "like your daddy used to do." Immediately he realized his mistake. "I'm sorry. I shouldn't have said that."

"It's all right. I'm a grown woman, not a child," she said quietly.

As if in acknowledgement, his gaze traveled over her form outlined beneath the sheet. Then he averted his eyes, opened the book and began to read — to her amazement — a love poem.

The resonant tone caressed the words, called out to her soul.

How about *The Rime of the Ancient Mariner* or *The Raven*, she wanted to shout out to break this spell he was casting over her with every line he recited, further fueling her desire. This is getting too dangerous, she commiserated.

Chad was monstrous to tantalize her like this, placing himself so near and yet so far. While he focused on the printed page, she stared at him, hypnotized, wondering when this sweet torture was going to end.

When he glanced up, turning the page, she quickly dropped her eyelids, feigning sleep. She hoped he was unaware that she'd been staring at him.

Suddenly, it seemed impossible to open them again. She drifted into sleep and in her dreams she saw a towering, muscular man with dark brown hair and expressive topaz eyes gazing lovingly at her.

Chapter 6

The brilliant colors of sunrise filtered through louvered windows, tinting the cottage a golden pink.

Barely awake, Denyse snuggled closely against something warm, firm, and wonderful. Her lips curved into the hint of a smile as she wrapped her arm around a broad, lightly furred chest, nuzzling her cheek against the shoulder where it was resting.

She sighed contentedly as she stretched lazily alongside the other form, then opened her eyes. From beneath slowly ascending lids, her gaze met a pair of brandy-colored eyes. The curve of her lips widened into a dazzling smile, returned in kind by the man of her dreams.

Then, as abruptly as if doused by a bucket of cold water, Denyse came fully alert. She catapulted away from an amused Chad. "Omigosh, I'm sorry."

"I'm not, for a change."

Denyse saw in a flash that Chad had remained partially clothed in the pale green slacks. He was lying on top of the bedspread.

"I stayed last night in case you needed anything else," Chad was saying. "I didn't expect a bonus."

Denyse realized with a start, although she'd remained between the sheets, only the lower portion of her body was still covered. She uttered a tiny, "Oh!" and grasped the sheet up around her neck, although she wanted to conceal her entire face which felt as pink as the sunrise.

"How are you feeling this morning?"

"Fine." She neglected to mention her quickened pulse and the sweet ache that had plagued her for much of the night.

"No more headache?"

"Not a bit."

"Sure?"

"Positive."

"Then I guess I can tell you what a cruel torture you are, Denyse. I've been watching you for the last hour, and thought I was going to have to tie my head to the bedpost to keep from kissing you here —" His mouth merged tenderly with hers, sampling, savoring. "And elsewhere," he added teasingly.

He leaned on one hand, while his other brushed strands of auburn hair away from her yearning face. His mouth hovered over hers as he reiterated, "Do you have any idea

106

how difficult it was not to kiss you, with your soft lips parted so invitingly . . ."

Again their lips locked and they moved into a closer embrace.

With a long sigh, Chad pulled away slightly. "You know, I didn't plan this, Denyse," he murmured.

"Neither of us did," she replied softly. "Are you sorry it's happening?"

"No, of course not." Yet he seemed to be struggling to regain control of himself again.

Denyse regarded him with a puzzled expression, feeling strangely bereft.

"Everything feels right about this," he said, "except we're going about it in the wrong order."

"The procedures seemed pretty okay to me," she half-joked. What the heck was he talking about? Why didn't he just shut up and kiss her again?

"Maybe I'm just a cliché kind of person. I suppose Wick would use the word uptight instead. But some of those old platitudes have merit, like business before pleasure. I've never improperly mingled the two."

Proper. Improper. *He* sounded like the one from Boston.

Denyse's gray eyes narrowed. She'd heard unlikely tales of women withholding sex as a means of obtaining something else, but she didn't know that could be a masculine ploy, too. Was this the price of liberation? Equivalent treatment from men?

Denyse had been planning to listen objectively to Chad's business proposal the next time he mentioned it, but if he thought he could manipulate her by dangling the prospect of his body thus far denied her —

Unaware of the new bent of her thoughts, Chad was continuing between ragged breaths, "More importantly, I don't want to ever leave anything unspoken between us. I know this isn't exactly the appropriate time or place for a business discussion —"

"The setting is a little" — she searched for the word — ". . . improper." She glanced at the sheet which was the only thing separating her from Chad. Think of the bed as a conference table with a peach-colored tablecloth, she told herself.

But her gaze journeyed from the sheet, back along the length of Chad's form as she remembered the strong legs beneath those green slacks. Her gaze moved along his enticing bare chest, his handsome face. Her eyes misted over dreamily when they again met his.

"Oh, Denyse." Chad slowly shook his head from side to side in near surrender. "Right now, those eyes definitely belong in a bedroom rather than a boardroom."

"I can't help it if I'm not bored at the moment," she punned.

"Me either." He leaned forward, bringing his lips an inch from hers before forcing himself with obvious effort to sit back up. "I know I should walk away from here this morning, for now. But I'm only human, and I'm not that strong —"

Chad swallowed hard and Denyse resisted an impulse to touch the pulsating area by his throat.

"Before we can go any further, I need to offer you five and a half million dollars."

She fluttered her eyelashes in exaggerated coquettishness, returning his teasing even though the interruption frustrated her. "Why, Chad, suh, I'm very flattered. But while I may be very good," she finished with an eminently seductive smile, half siren, half imp, "even I don't figure I'm worth five and a half million dollars."

"Oh, I think maybe you are." Chad grinned back, absently reaching up and tracing her lips with a gentle finger before he realized what he was doing and jerked his hand back.

"I'm serious, Denyse," he said. "I'm representing a real estate development syndicate that wants to buy Sunrise Key. Their latest offer is five and a half million dollars."

Denyse dissolved into a gale of laughter.

"I'm not kidding, Denyse," Chad said. When her laughter continued, he added, somewhat chagrined, "You can get your own appraisal, of course —"

"It's not that," she finally managed to say. "I thought you wanted to sell me paper clips and typewriter ribbons, or maybe printed napkins or frozen cheesecake for the dining room."

Chad joined in the mirth. Then said in a more serious tone, "Didn't you read the card I gave you — CTJ Associates, Real Estate Sales and Development."

"I put the card in my purse without ever really looking at it."

She sat up, trying to produce more of a businesslike demeanor. She gathered the peach-colored sheet around her. "Sorry I don't have pinstriped sheets," she remarked, then couldn't help giggling again. They were actually preparing to discuss a five-and-a-half-million-dollar business deal while sitting in the middle of the bed, half undressed.

Chad continued, "We don't have to sign contracts this very minute, I just thought you should know my reason for coming here the other night. I didn't want you to feel —"

He fumbled for the word.

"Used," she supplied.

"Certainly not used," he said. "Not even insufficiently informed. I don't ever want secrets of any kind between us." But he glanced away as he made that statement, not meeting her eyes, causing her to wonder for an instant if other secrets remained between them.

Five million plus dollars on a check made out in her own name boggled her mind. There might even be a something worthwhile left after taxes. She'd known Sunrise Key was worth a good deal of money if it wasn't mortgaged to the hilt, but for all she knew, it was. She hadn't yet had a chance to assess the assets and liabilities. Other things had seemed more pressing to her.

"To bring the business aspect of today's discussion to a temporary conclusion," she began in the most professional tone she could muster, "naturally, I've considered selling Sunrise Key. But that's only one of my options — although I'd never have known I'd have a buyer so quickly and so easily. But I haven't finished a basic financial analysis yet, much less made any major decisions."

Briefly, she wondered if he might be romancing her to get her signature on the dotted line. It seemed unlikely, though. Besides, she simply couldn't face any possibility that Chad's interest in her, however shallow and fleeting it might be, wasn't at least genuine.

She added jestingly in a businesslike dismissal, hoping he understood it was only the business she was dismissing, "I'll notify you if and when I'm ready to sell, Mr. — Mr. —" Jarringly, she realized aloud, "Hey, I don't even know your last name."

"My name's on my card," he bantered.

"Then would you mind bringing me my purse? I think it's in my office."

"Mmmm," he considered. "I'm not inclined to abandon my current strategic position right here." He gave her a formal nod of his handsome head. "Mr. Chadwick at your service."

"Chad Chadwick?"

"Not exactly. Donald Ronald Chadwick, to be precise."

"Donald Ronald?" She giggled again.

"That, Ms. Benton, is why I go by Chad. Actually, I think my father was a frustrated poet. And rightly frustrated since he named my brother Daniel Randall. Our early nicknames were Don and Dan, but of course we were never sure which of us was being summoned — or so we pretended when we didn't want to answer. When we were teen-agers, each struggling for our own adolescent identities, the confusion became more of a problem for us. So, with the wisdom of Solomon, we simply divided our last name in half."

Chad's fingers enveloped and squeezed hers, and they sat in silence for a while. Denyse again wondered about Chad's motives. She couldn't imagine Chad doing anything not totally aboveboard. Or maybe she just didn't want to.

For now, Chad's fingers lightly brushing her hand postponed further concentration on that or most everything else for that matter.

Chad eventually broke the silence. "Wick and I are so different," he said, distractedly. "Everybody considers me the straightlaced businessman in the three-piece suit — figuratively speaking of course because nobody in his right mind would wear a three-piece suit in Florida. Wick, on the other hand, is the modern version of the romantic swash-buckler."

"So he told me."

Chad digested that piece of information. "It's sort of true. Most women could lose their hearts to him in a matter of minutes." His comment was more a question than a statement.

She squeezed his hand. "CPAs from Boston are crazy about three-piece suits, especially when a certain attractive man is only wearing one figuratively."

"Sure I'm not just a substitute for my more dashing but absent brother?"

Chad spoke with a grin, but she detected an undertone of actual insecurity that twisted her heart with tenderness. It had never occurred to her that someone as charming, attractive, and confident as Chad, could wonder whether he was wanted totally for himself. Just as she had been wondering, she realized abruptly, whether he wanted her for herself or for some ulterior motive.

It was time for them to trust each other, and for her to have faith in her own instincts.

"Brother?" she said to reassure him. "I don't remember any brother. In fact, I can't seem to bring to mind any other male in the entire world except you."

Chad lifted her hand to his lips, bestowing a series of kisses along the back, on each fingertip, on the sensitive center of her palm.

"Does this mean our business meeting is adjourned?" she asked huskily, as the fires which had never ceased to smolder within her were fueled more, threatening to blaze beyond control.

He moved her hand higher, trapping it lovingly against his cheek. "There is another matter we ought to discuss."

She sighed. "Well, go ahead, Mr. Chadwick."

"Of a personal nature, Denyse." He gave her a half smile.

"Okay," she answered, puzzled.

"Did you really mean it when you said you don't want to have children?" His question came slowly, notched with hesitation.

"Chad, not too many women want to have illegitimate children."

"I know. But, I mean . . . ever?"

She'd thought her decision was made. She was ninety-nine percent certain. She squirmed under his scrutiny. Was the man shopping for a baby factory? Finally, she answered, "I enjoy my career. I don't think I have the patience to deal with small humans and domestic routines." Her eyes beseeched him to accept that.

Frustration and puzzlement mingled and she added with a smidgen of annoyance, "Why are we having this discussion now? Isn't this a little early in our relationship — if this can even be called a relationship?"

"I'd call it that, and maybe more." His

fingertip traced the outline of her face. "I'm not into short, casual flings, and I don't think you are either."

"No," she murmured, toasty inside that he had sensed that without her telling him so. But the original point of this discussion wasn't lost on her. Her next statement was more a lament than a question. "So you don't want to become involved with a woman who's not interested in marriage and children?"

"I want what you want."

A sunburst was set ablaze within her. She couldn't believe she'd heard him correctly. "What?" she whispered.

He kissed the tip of her nose gently. "I think I might be falling in love with you."

"I think I might be falling in love with you, too." The words slipped through her lips, seemingly of their own volition.

She'd felt last night that she might be falling in love with Chad, but she'd denied it to herself, manufacturing an array of reasons: Their time together had been too short. She didn't really know him.

But the main reason was that she didn't think it possible that he could be falling in love with her.

I think I might be, he'd said.

And he certainly hadn't had to say that to

116

get her into bed. She was already there and straining at the sheet.

A discussion of future children need take place only if there was a possibility of a future.

Those and all other thoughts were driven from her mind as quickly as a puff of wind could scatter autumn leaves, when Chad drew her more tightly into one arm and slipped the other beneath the sheet.

His amber eyes reminded her of cherished autumns in New England as his body shifted above hers.

But there was nothing cool or crisp in her responses. Tiny flames ignited beneath his slow caresses. His mouth and tongue followed his hands along her flesh and fanned the fires singeing every cell of her being.

"Chad, Chad —" she purred from deep within her throat.

She clenched and stroked the muscles of his chest and back, then glided her hands along his ribs, caressing him.

Her questing fingers dropped to his trousers and sought to free the evidence of his passion.

"Oh, Denyse," he moaned, replacing the lacy scrap of her panties with his hand.

She writhed in ecstasy as his fingers brought her pleasure that began with a tremor at her core, then sent shock waves throughout her being.

"Denyse, my darling . . ."

His mouth locked onto hers and he spread her thighs gently apart.

His penetration sent her soaring to heights she'd never known existed. She pulled him tight against her, wanting to feel the exciting pressure of him in every way. His strokes deepened as they breathed in harmony, sighing each other's names. The world was left behind as they moved in their own sphere. They swirled, locked together, toward a distant, fiery sun.

Chapter 7

Hours later, Denyse stood inside the open cottage doorway swathed in the yellow silk kimono that Chad had given her in the hospital.

She was also wrapped in Chad, who was fully dressed. Neither of them was in a rush to end the embrace.

"I wish this darned lunch appointment wasn't so important," Chad said for the sixth time.

"It's okay."

"Now that I know what I've been missing in the daytime, I'll never make a lunch appointment again."

"Just make sure you eat sometime," Denyse said. "It's important to keep up your strength."

"We'll work on that together at dinner. I'll stop at one of my favorite restaurants on Captiva and bring home shrimp and all the trimmings for two."

Home. He already was thinking of her as home, she realized, and love took deeper root within her heart.

"Maybe I could toss a couple of gypsy violinists aboard the cabin cruiser, too. In case we need them."

"I don't think we need them," she replied with a laugh.

He dropped a quick kiss on the tip of her nose. "All afternoon I'll hold the image in my mind of you waiting at the cottage door. I have to go now," he said without moving.

"Uh-huh," she agreed.

"On the count of three," he pronounced eventually. "One . . . two . . ."

Three never came, as he melded his mouth to hers, once again exploring those honeyed recesses with his tongue.

A deep, sardonic voice intruded. "Looks like I stayed away too long."

Chad and Denyse didn't exactly spring apart like errant teenagers. Chad turned, keeping his arm loosely around her shoulders.

"Uh, hi, Wick —" she was starting to say.

Chad came directly to the point. "I'd like to think it wouldn't have made a difference whether you were here or not."

"Maybe the lady would have selected differently if she'd known all her choices," Wick replied to Chad, ignoring Denyse.

That fueled a response of her own. "That lady has a name, Wick, as I've pointed out several times. What did you think? That I considered the two of you parts of a bachelor smorgasbord that I had to choose from?" She swallowed further words, realizing she had been close to thinking that when she'd first arrived — not *had* to choose, but wanted to.

Wick, dressed in his usual jeans and shirt, affected a sweeping bow. "My apologies, Milady Denyse. Or, I guess I should say, His Lady Denyse. Obviously, Chad made you an offer you couldn't refuse. More than one offer apparently."

Denyse directed her question to Chad, finding herself speaking of Wick in the same type of third-person reference she'd just objected to. "Does he know about the real estate —"

Wick, as usual, interrupted. "I know about the seven-million-dollar offer for Sunrise Key. Your father rejected that many times."

"*Seven* million?" Denyse hardly needed a calculator or a CPA license to figure out that a million and a half dollars had disappeared somewhere along the way.

Chad's arm tightened around her stiffening shoulders, but she pulled away, turning to face him.

"Is he talking about the same buyer?" she asked softly, as if a gentle tone would be more likely to elicit the answer she wanted to hear.

"Yes," Chad admitted on a sigh. "But you have to understand that I'm only the middleman, responsible for passing on the offers as presented to me. The original offer was five million. That was periodically raised over the course of a year, so their last offer to your father was seven million."

"I see."

"No, you don't," Chad said sadly, seeing a veil pass over her eyes. "They had become so eager to buy Sunrise Key from your father that their last offer was at least a million too high."

"Even if true, that would leave a small matter of half a million unaccounted for."

"You can always negotiate, Denyse. You know that. You can get your own appraisal and we can take it from there."

"I suppose the last few days, last night especially, wasn't intended to shade my thinking."

"You know better than that. Your business judgment isn't clouded, is it?"

"No." She added in a mumble, "Only my personal judgment."

"*Whoa,*" Chad said. "We agreed to keep business and personal matters separate. I was honest with you, before . . . before . . ." He glanced at Wick. ". . . well, you know."

"Yes, you did tell me, eventually." When

you were sure my hormones wouldn't let me turn back, she thought unreasonably.

Chad reached out to pull her into his arms, but she wriggled out of his grasp.

"Last night, I laughed when I thought you were teasing me with an offer of five and a half million, and told you I wasn't worth it. Well, let me tell you, Mr. Chadwick, if you thought you were worth a million and a half, you need some new appraisals yourself." Her voice caught.

His jawline clenched as he struggled to maintain control. "I thought I was dealing with a mature woman, in bed and out."

"Dealing?" she flung the word back at him.

"Stop this." It wasn't exactly a yell, but it was a couple of decibels higher than the tone he'd managed before.

Peripherally, she wondered how much more it would take to goad him into shouting. She felt like screaming herself. Yelling. Blowing the fronds off the palm trees with the timbre of her voice.

She did stop, however, for a few moments. He had been accurate on one point. She was a mature woman, and she'd recognized all along that her mental well-being was at risk if she let her passion take over.

She grew outwardly calm. He'd been correct on another point also.

"You were right that first night," she told him, as soon as she could dredge the words out of her constricted throat. "We should have gotten the business out of the way before the pleasure. Now we'll have to forget that we had a temporary detour."

"Denyse —" he began in a pleading but dignified tone.

"That caveat was yours. I should have heeded it."

"Caveat emptor. Let the buyer beware. I don't know the Latin phrase for 'let the buyer's representative beware.' "

"And I don't know the Latin phrase for 'let the seller beware.' But the seller — potential seller," she amended, "intends to be wary from now on."

"Denyse, please don't do this to us."

"If there is an 'us,' the us shouldn't mind waiting until all this is settled."

"Speak for your half of the us only," he grumbled. "But if that's the way you want it —"

No. What she wanted was to turn back the clock to a very recent time when Chad and she had been as one. *Seemed* as one, she mentally corrected herself.

Why couldn't he have told her about the earlier offers? Because it would have been a breach of professional ethics, she explained to herself. But what was sharing a bed with a potential seller?

One was business. One was personal. She tried to convince herself of that.

"I still need to complete a basic financial and management analysis before I decide whether to consider any *and all* offers," she managed to say rather haughtily. "I'll call your office in a week or so and we can make an appointment to discuss this. Perhaps," she couldn't resist adding, "you'll have to break your new vow not to have lunch appointments. My thinking seems clearest around midday."

No longer patient, Chad pivoted away. A shell shattered under his heel. "Whenever, whatever, you say."

Chad's eyes flung daggers at Wick who had remained uncharacteristically silent, but who looked pleased by the conversation on which he'd so openly eavesdropped. "Thanks a bunch."

"Any time, brother dear," Wick replied irreverently.

Chad strode angrily away and Wick moved closer to Denyse. "Need a shoulder to cry on?" he offered.

"I have two of my own."

"An extra always comes in handy."

"I nev . . . nev . . . never cry," she informed him, ignoring the tears streaking down her face.

"Denyse, I'm sorry if —" Wick began.

"Don't you start apologizing and being nice to me, too," she countered irascibly. "Just leave me alone."

"I was only trying to help."

"Oh, go pillage a village or something." She waved him away, slamming and locking the cottage door.

Two days later, Denyse returned to her office after a restless post-lunch stroll on the beach. Scattered atop her desk were a giant heart-shaped box of candy, a cluster of daisies, and a thin volume which at a closer glance proved to be a book of poetry.

The embers still smoldering within her glowed more brightly, even as she prepared to complain to Chad about failing to honor his agreement to await her call.

She saw to her amazement, however, that the man ensconced in the burgundy leather chair in the corner wasn't Chad, but Wick.

"What is all this?" Surprise reflected in her voice.

"I pillaged a village and came up with that?"

"Sure." She crossed to her desk and sat

behind it, absently placing a barrier between them. "Why bring your booty here?"

"Well . . . you . . ."

She wouldn't have expected Wick to be shy. Just the opposite. So he must be embarrassed. Trying to pull something off that his heart wasn't into. Her eyes narrowed. "No, I don't know. Confess."

"Well," he said with what might have been uncertainty for the first time in his life. "I sort of thought that was the type of stuff Chad would bring."

"Actually, he brought roses, lipstick, a hairbrush, a bathrobe, a pareo, a skirt, a blouse, and peppermint-flavored toothpaste," she catalogued.

"Huh?"

"At the hospital." She picked up the daisies, then put them back down. "As regards the mystery of a Sneak Bearing Gifts . . ."

"Don't be insulting. I'm only a part-time sneak."

She ignored his protest, continuing, ". . . we have the what, where, and who. What's missing is the" — she directed a piercing stare at him — "why."

"Well, you know . . ." he started again, but her look reminded him that she didn't. He finally said, "I'm courting."

"Courting?" She couldn't hold back a

chuckle. "Where did you spend the last few days? A time warp in the Bermuda Triangle?"

He doo-dahed the television theme song associated with Rod Serling.

"That was the Twilight Zone. Not the Bermuda Triangle."

"I must have gotten my navigation off course."

"I'd say your navigation was off course when you came here with a heart-shaped box of chocolates." It wasn't like her to be inconsiderate of another person's feelings, but she couldn't take Wick's romantic overtures seriously, especially since she doubted that he did.

"I'm getting the impression here that maybe you think we aren't meant for each other," he said.

"I'd say that sums it up. In addition to which, you already know I'm involved with your brother. Is that what this is about? Sibling rivalry? Being your brother's lover's keeper?"

"No." His sea-blue eyes met hers. "It just seems like it should have been, maybe still should be, you and me."

"Why?" she repeated.

"For starters, you *are* Dennis's daughter . . ."

"And nothing like him, as near as I can figure out. You don't know me well enough to be seriously interested in me. In fact, everything we know about each other stacks together as a monument to why we could never fall in love."

"Not everything." He gave her a rakish grin. The grin faded. "Was I wrong to sense some mutual attraction that first day, that night when I kissed you?"

"Not exactly," she admitted. "But it would never have held up for long. We're too different."

"You think you and Chad are eternally destined?"

After a pause, she answered, "Your guess would be more valid than mine." Again, she attempted to pin him with an interrogating stare. "If I sell to his clients, he'll have a fat commission."

"I hate to be the bearer of depressing news," Wick interrupted. "Especially since I'm the one it's depressing." He gazed out the window for a moment before continuing. "The commission wouldn't be that important to Chad. He's built a respectable fortune already."

Denyse was tempted to ask Wick his definition of respectable. She hadn't confronted and dealt with all the matters facing her yet.

In fact, she hadn't even worked up the nerve to go back into the swamp and check out the cinder block building, sheepishly fearful for her own safety as well as wanting to avoid whatever unwelcome answers might await there.

Chad had done a good job of holding business at bay in her thoughts. But there were instances where Chad and business overlapped. "If he made the sale and dumped me, he'd only get the commission. But if I sold and he married me, he'd be getting a wife with a sizable dowry."

Wick let out a low whistle. "Wow. You two progressed that far in a few days? I've never known Chad to move that fast."

"What does that mean?"

"He isn't inclined toward quick or shallow involvements. There was only once —"

Denyse ached to ask Wick to relate the story of that once upon a time. But her pride prevailed.

Wick interrupted himself, gazing at Denyse with a renewed but different interest. "You two actually discussed marriage?"

"Not really. Only in general terms."

"To be honest," Wick said, "money's not that important to Chad. He just amassed it by being good at what he does."

"Maybe being good at what he does means closing the deal. Maybe it's a matter of professional pride to convince me to sell. Or maybe he's into power. Maybe he's one of the investors in the real-estate syndicate that wants to develop the island."

Wick pondered that. "I don't think so," he said finally, but his words were hesitant.

Denyse didn't add that Wick himself could fit any of the descriptions applied to Chad. He could be pretending opposition to the real estate development to throw her off guard, but actually expect to be cut in somehow. This surface rivalry could be a psychological game played for her benefit, a variation on the good cop–bad cop routine.

The possibilities were endless, especially given all the other unanswered questions about Wick and Chad's activities.

The one possibility she wanted to cling to was the least likely. Though she couldn't put any more store in Wick's response than if she'd written to an advice columnist, she couldn't help asking, "Do you believe Chad would romance me, make —" The words stuck to her tonsils before she could dislodge them. ". . . make love to me," she said with difficulty, "for a business deal?"

The pause before Wick replied seemed

like an eternity. "It would simplify my life a whole lot to answer yes to that question," Wick said finally. "But you are Dennis's daughter, so my honest answer to that question is no. Chad has separated business from pleasure for a long time, ever since —" He caught himself.

For a moment, Denyse's heart sang. But maybe Wick didn't know his brother that well; they certainly seemed at odds much of the time. Or perhaps Wick was lying to salvage her feelings out of respect for her father.

Wick adopted his usual jaunty attitude. "So my courtship is hopeless?"

" 'Fraid so."

"Then, are you on a diet?"

"Are you suggesting that I should lose weight?"

"You look fine to me. But most women are on a diet most of the time anyway. So if you aren't going to eat the chocolates —"

"You want them back?" She matched his grin. "For Porque?"

"Not unless I get thrown out of the next parlor, too," he admitted.

"Want the daisies back, too?"

"Only if you're allergic or something."

"I feel a sneeze coming on." She loaded the cheery blooms on top of the candy box and handed them to him. Her gaze fell on the book. "The poetry?"

"Only if you can't read because you've lost your glasses, or something like that."

"I feel an astigmatism coming on." She picked up the volume and rose from her chair. "I don't know if you can manage to return all this booty to the boat by yourself. I'll carry this down for you."

"Need a walk, huh?"

"Right," she lied, having not mentioned that she'd just returned from a stroll on the beach. She welcomed the opportunity to get another look at the boat to see if she could pick up on any clandestine clues.

She'd learned nothing at Wick's boat that day, nor in the days to follow. Porque scurried away whenever she approached, and Pablo, the First Mate, claimed he didn't speak English. She still hadn't even had a full tour of the boat, nor ventured back through the swamp.

She was glad to have Wick's frequent company, but she never lost sight of the fact that she couldn't completely trust him.

In her office one afternoon, she sat holding the phone, the receiver weighing heavily in her hands as it had done so many times when she'd lifted it, thinking of calling Chad. She'd always managed to hang up without dialing.

This time, though, she gave a long sigh and punched in a long-distance number. Her friend, Kelly Nyles Granger, had been coming to mind more and more lately and she finally decided to call her for advice.

Kelly and Denyse had met years ago when they were both young and wide-eyed, attending their first professional accounting conference in Miami, and they'd become fast friends.

Kelly would be the right person to advise her on a romance.

Even as she dialed Kelly's number, Denyse realized she was the one most likely to tell her what she wanted to hear: that love could strike fast, like a bolt of lightning, and still be everlasting.

Besides, Kelly was a financial consultant. Maybe she'd see some angles that had eluded Denyse, especially since her thinking wasn't its most reliable lately.

An hour later, Kelly was updated on all the details, business and personal, and Denyse wrapped it up by saying, "I need to find the top real-estate consultant in the area to advise me, but whenever I ask around the same name comes up — Chad Chadwick of CTJ Associates."

"There have to be other competent people in the area," Kelly said reasonably. "Consult more than one. Get a good consensus. You should do that anyway."

"I know." Denyse sighed. "The problem is, this one is filling up my entire mind."

"And your heart," Kelly said with the understanding of one who'd experienced the same feelings.

"Yes." She drew in a deep breath. "But I need to stop thinking of taxing men, and start figuring out what to do about inheritance taxes. Like I told you, my father had been refinancing the mortgage every year for the last few years to pay the property tax, basic upkeep, and salaries — although the expenses seem way out of line with the reported revenues. But if he was skimming revenues, I don't know what he did with the profits. They must be hidden in some numbered Swiss bank account, where they'll remain forever undiscovered."

"You're sure about the revenue gap?"

"Absolutely. Expenses have way outpaced the reported number of guests at the resort. And that's not counting the other revenue disparity that I have figured out."

"There's more?"

"Burt, the accountant and office manager, has been blatantly embezzling for several years. No wonder the resort didn't have enough money for personnel and upkeep, so it lost customers and got into even deeper financial trouble. Burt had no finesse. I can't imagine how my father never caught on."

They talked more. Finally, Denyse summed up, "By the time I have to pay the first installment on the inheritance tax, I'll have to either sell the whole island or figure a way to make it pay fast. I can remortgage for operating funds for a while, like my father kept doing. But there's no point if I can't make enough money to make it pay in the long run. I'd just wind up further in the red, maybe forced into some type of sacrifice sale at a lower price."

She'd been leaning back in the desk chair with her feet up on the credenza. She lowered her feet to the floor, and began to swivel back around toward the desk, continuing her discourse. "If my father couldn't make it pay with all his years of experience, what makes me think I can? Of course, he appears to have been somewhat careless in recent years, but he did build this place from scratch in the beginning, so maybe the hard times weren't all his fault . . ."

As she swiveled around in the chair, she saw Wick standing just inside the office door. She'd forgotten his propensity for silent entrances. Maybe she'd have to start locking her office, too, even when she was in it.

"Kelly, someone's come into my office, so I'll have to cut this short."

"Call whenever you want someone to talk to," her friend reminded her. "And if you want me to come and help, let me know. I can be on a plane if you need me."

"Thanks, Kelly. That means a lot to me. I think I've got it as under control as I can, but I'll keep in touch, maybe bounce some more ideas off on you."

Denyse's eyes never wavered from Wick while she exchanged good-byes with Kelly.

"Well?" she challenged upon hanging up.

"What?"

She sighed. He was hopelessly irrepressible, and that word didn't have nearly as many positive connotations as she'd once associated it with. "Don't you ever knock?"

"No."

"So how long have you been standing there listening?"

"I wasn't trying to eavesdrop, Denyse. I came in to see you and I couldn't help but overhear a part of your call."

"Well, what did you overhear while you were just standing there not really listening but unable to stop yourself from over-hearing?"

"Inheritance taxes. Burt." Despite his casual tone, his usual jauntiness wasn't evident.

She wondered if he'd also heard her outpouring over Chad.

"By the way," Wick said with a trace of the old sarcasm, "your father wasn't an incompetent."

It wasn't a point she wanted to argue, in light of heredity and all. "Maybe he just didn't have a head for business."

"As you pointed out, he built this resort from nothing into a great success."

"Then let it go downhill."

"Downhill is all a matter of opinion," Wick mumbled. After a pause, he added, "The inheritance taxes have me worried."

"You? I don't think the bill will come in under your name."

"I mean, worried for you."

But she sensed that wasn't what he'd meant at all. Why should Wick worry about the inheritance taxes on Sunrise Key?

He voluntarily explained without her having to ask the question. "Like I told you, Dennis didn't want to sell to developers. I don't want you to have to either."

"There may be other options."

"I sure hope you can come up with some. Too bad my brilliant brother is on the other side."

The other side. Not beside her where he belonged, but opposite her. Denyse's heart wrenched at the reminder.

"A little hurricane would be nice," she said, attempting lightness. "Something that would hit Sunrise Key and damage all the buildings except whichever one we're all safe inside. Just enough to collect the insurance for refurbishment. I don't suppose you could conjure up a mini hurricane?"

"I've been accused of stirring up a few storms in my time," Wick replied, "but I think that's beyond me." His smile faded and he again appeared genuinely distressed. "What else can you do, really?"

"I've got a few ideas." She hadn't planned to share them with Wick, still not trusting him with confidences, but she was surprised he didn't press for details.

He was otherwise absorbed, his tanned brow furrowing above the sea-blue eyes. "What are you going to do about Burt?"

"Promise not to tell?" Wick would be the last person to warn Burt, she figured. He became visibly agitated whenever Burt was in the vicinity.

"Cross my heart."

"I'm having Carlos chauffeur me in the motorboat tomorrow. I'll be talking to the district attorney about criminal prosecution."

Wick's eyes reflected, to her surprise, not anger but anguish. "Wait, please," he said. "Please wait a few days."

"*What?*" she asked in disbelief. Please? Twice? In two consecutive sentences? *From Wick?*

She had to give this some consideration. Any alien casually dropping in from outer space and totally unschooled in human behavior could have discerned there was no affection between Wick and Burt. Why was Wick pleading Burt's case?

"Please wait, just until the middle of next week."

"Why?"

"Trust me."

Not a chance. If she wasn't going to trust Chad, she certainly wouldn't cast her lot with Wick.

Reading the answer in her face, Wick said, "I'm no fan of Burt's. But I was your father's friend. Please believe me when I tell you that this would have been okay with him, the way he would have wanted it."

So Wick didn't want the authorities poking around the island. Had her father been involved? Or had Wick been using him, as he or Chad might be trying to use her?

Whatever Wick was up to, and even if his friendliness was an act, he was the brother of the man she loved.

She refused to dwell on the possibility that Chad might be involved, too. Had Sunrise Key made an unwitting contribution toward his "respectable" fortune?

"I'll wait until Tuesday to turn Burt in," she agreed reluctantly.

"Tuesday. Well, that's something." He seemed to be doing quick calculations in his mind.

"In the meantime, I'm contacting the banks to cancel Burt's check-signing authorization. I'll hold off on the criminal charges, but I'm not giving him a chance to add to his loot."

"Fine with me."

"And Wick," she said, giving him fair warning, "I'll be keeping a much closer eye on everything that goes on on Sunrise Key than my father did. Any and all illegal activities will be reported to the authorities."

His blue gaze reflected comprehension.

Chapter 8

Wearing an insincere smile, Denyse told Burt the next morning, "Gee, maybe you were right. There are some things here I don't understand. I've never worked in this kind of business before." She feigned a helpless, girlish look. "If you haven't accepted another position yet, maybe you wouldn't mind staying on here for a while."

She held back a gag at his smug, superior expression. "Sure, Ms. Benton. Anything I can do to help. I've been here a long time."

"Not quite long enough, it seems. But I know you were expecting some free time, and you have been working awfully hard." She noticed a narrowing of his eyes. If she laid it on too thick, he'd get suspicious. "Since the resort's not busy now — Gee, I hope it picks up somehow during winter season — Maybe you'd like to take a few days off. With pay, of course. I'm so grateful that you'll be able to stay on."

"Well, I do have some paid vacation coming —" He started slowly, unable to analyze all the angles just yet.

"Oh, you figure out the payroll and benefits. I'll leave the details to you."

"It's not more than a few days I have coming," he said, still regarding her skeptically.

"That's wonderful. At least from my viewpoint. I'd like to have you available in case I need advice. Would it be too much trouble for you to be back at work next Wednesday?"

"I'll be here, bright and early."

Early, maybe. But not bright, she thought triumphantly. His assumption that a woman couldn't handle business was allaying his suspicions of her motives.

She proceeded with her plans for the rest of the day, omitting only the district attorney's office since she'd promised Wick to wait until Tuesday. In the meantime, Burt wouldn't be around to write any checks.

She'd learned that the resort kept a car on Captiva, so Carlos had to take her only that far in the motorboat.

Her first stop was at the local bank handling her business accounts. She deleted Burt's signature from the authorization to sign checks, speaking directly to the bank's manager to ensure nothing would accidentally pass through.

Then she found the boutique, Dressed for Excess, to exchange her skirt and blouse for the right sizes, buoyed by Wick's opinion that Chad wouldn't have romanced her for business reasons. In any case, she thought she might wear this outfit at some future time to titillate him if his affection was sincere or maybe taunt him with what he had lost if it was not.

Instead, as she stroked the fabric she found she was taunting herself, imagining the ways Chad could undress her.

The salesclerk cheerfully disappeared to find the right sizes. She exchanged her clothes and headed toward the car.

The far horizon was swathed in a fiery orange by the time she'd driven back to the far end of Captiva. She needed to telephone Carlos to meet her with the motorboat.

Chad's condo was only a couple of blocks from the garage where she needed to leave the car. Somehow that seemed much more convenient than the closer public telephone on the corner. She wondered whether he'd be home. Perhaps the repainting wasn't completed yet, and he was still staying in Fort Myers every night.

She wanted to see him. She needed to see him. It was as simple as that, no matter how many ways she tried to justify why her legs were rapidly taking her in that direction.

She recognized the elegant building; its location had been etched in her memory when he'd pointed it out to her. As she scanned the directory for Chad's apartment number, she saw a familiar name and blinked. One of the tenants listed was Burt Johnson.

No way could his salary cover the price of a place like this. Denyse knew how he'd been able to afford it — family money, *her* family money. He'd been blatant enough to spend his skimmings so close by and so obviously.

She walked through the lobby and into a spacious courtyard spouting palm trees and colorful tropical plants surrounded by the apartments.

Her mind was in turmoil. Wouldn't Chad have suspected Burt, knowing that he'd bought such an expensive condo? Maybe Burt had claimed to have inherited money, she wanted to believe, and Chad had no reason to check into it.

Or did Burt's living near Chad mean something even more? Something too wrenching to even contemplate.

She paused, upset and confused. Her gaze fell on Chad's apartment. Tonight wouldn't be a good time to see him. Yet she found herself climbing the open staircase to the second floor.

Chimes sounded within when she pressed

the doorbell, and a beautiful, petite woman answered the door. "Yes?" There was a smile in the woman's voice as well as on her lips. She wore a yellow silk kimono modestly tied. A different sort of tie was displayed in the double set of diamond rings, glimmering like daggers from her third finger, left hand.

From within was the sound of a shower, barely muffling a man's hearty baritone.

Denyse could only stand there in shock. Maybe — just maybe — she had the wrong apartment. She grasped at that hope. "Is this Mr. Chadwick's apartment?" Her voice suddenly sounded very small.

"Yes, it is. Was he expecting you?" she asked in a friendly manner.

"Well, uh, no. I was in the neighborhood and thought I'd drop in." *I can't believe I said that,* she thought. "We've been discussing some business," she added quickly.

"He's not available right now. Would you like to come in and wait?"

What I'd like to do is throw Mr. Chadwick off the balcony. Preferably something higher than the second floor.

When she didn't answer immediately, the redheaded woman prompted, "My husband's in the shower, but you shouldn't have to tolerate his caterwauling too much longer."

Husband . . . Denyse made one last-ditch attempt to alter the reality of the situation. "This is the same Chadwick who owns CTJ Associates?"

"The very one."

So this charming lady was the "re-painting," the reason why Chad wouldn't bring her here. Rage boiled through her, along with an anguish that left her so weak she could scarcely speak.

"Thank you." She heard a disembodied voice similar to hers saying, "I believe I will wait."

She didn't want to hurt this lovely woman, who would be tormented soon enough when she learned about the methods her husband employed to drum up business. But it might be well worth it to see Chad's face when he saw the woman he "thought he might be falling in love with" sitting next to his wife.

She took in the spacious living room with its airy decor fashioned of pale driftwood and cypress amid comfortable furniture in tropical colors. In the best of taste. Decorated, no doubt, by Chad's wife. I have no idea what I'm doing sitting here, she thought.

But she *did* have business with him. Business that could now be dispensed with very quickly.

She would tell him — with relish no matter how much it might cost her — that under no circumstances would she ever sell to any client of CTJ Associates.

She accepted the glass of ice tea offered by her congenial, unsuspecting hostess, who was saying, "I'm a partner in the company, so I won't have to scurry out of the way for your discussion." She laughed. "I was a commercial real-estate broker and business partner before I was a wife."

At least he had kept the business and pleasure in strict order here.

"Are you possibly Denyse Benton?" she asked.

"Oh," Denyse responded, startled. "Yes. I'm sorry. I forgot to introduce myself."

"Chad's been talking about you —"

"He has?" The words rocketed out of her.

"In fact, I confess to teasing him about it. Especially since he hardly ever uses words like 'beautiful' to describe a business contact."

She really couldn't handle this. She had to get out of here. "Thank you for the tea, but I don't believe I'll wait after all."

"Please do. It shouldn't be long —" As if on cue, the sound of the shower stopped and she called out, "Come out decent, darling. We have company."

I wouldn't be seeing anything I haven't seen before, Denyse thought.

But she was wrong. She was seeing something she hadn't seen before.

The man who emerged from the shower wrapped in a terry robe wasn't Chad, but a stranger.

"This is Denyse Benton," her hostess was saying. "Denyse, this is my soggy husband, Ramon Tomas. He's the 'T' in CTJ Associates. And I guess I haven't introduced myself either. I'm the 'J,' Nicole Jamison."

"Nicole Jamison Tomas now," her husband mumbled, apparently ribbing her on a source of contention between them. "Hello, Denyse." His voice held the trace of an accent. The Hispanic man, a couple of inches shorter than Denyse, crossed the room and offered his hand. "So you're the one Chad's been talking about so much."

"Nice to meet you," she said, too emotionally drained to manage more than that.

"Chad should be here soon," he added. "He loaned us the use of this place while the house we bought is being remodeled. We're having dinner to discuss all our current projects —" He stopped himself. "But that can wait. We'd all much rather have you join us for dinner."

"Yes," Nicole urged.

"Thank you, but I really only dropped by for a minute." Or a lifetime.

She had far too much to sort out before seeing Chad again, for business or pleasure. She'd known that before she even came to his condo. Being flattened by a few emotional steamrollers was exactly what she deserved for being impulsive and foolish.

She rose and started toward the door. "I was nearby, and was just going to tell Chad that I haven't made any decisions yet. Please tell him I'll call him at the office in a week or so."

She was restless that night. It was hot, steaming, despite the incessant drone of the air conditioner. She couldn't sleep.

At the first hint of dawn, Denyse got out of bed and took a quick shower. Perversely, she dressed in the full-tiered red skirt and scoop-necked white peasant blouse, then strapped on her sandals, planning to walk off her frustration and confusion.

Dawn pearled the horizon as she set off for the beach, opting for the shell-strewn shore. For once, the occasional crunch of shells beneath her foot provided a sort of companionable accompaniment for her restless rovings.

The ocean provided a soft symphony of

ever-changing rhythms — whispering seductively, roaring demandingly — just as her body reacted to Chad.

Like her, the sea reached out, inched forward, then pulled back — uncertain whether these shores offered refuge and peace.

Suddenly he was there.

Chad appeared through the morning mist, conjured by her fantasies.

She'd been seeing his face, his form, in her sleep for the past several nights. She couldn't believe that he was real, as though placed upon the shore for her to view, to enjoy — maybe even to touch.

They walked toward one another slowly, cautiously, as if each were afraid they were gazing on a mirage.

"It really is you," she said.

"I thought I'd imagined you," he murmured. He reached out, his fingertips like butterfly wings. "So you like the outfit?"

"Very much," she managed to answer, though her throat felt constricted at his touch.

He wore white jeans and a teal-blue shirt that billowed in the stirrings of the ocean breeze.

Her mind refused to consider all the reasons why he might be on Sunrise Key at such an early hour. Nonetheless, she asked, "Why are you here?"

"Nicole told me you dropped by last night."

"But I said I'd call your office later." It was a quiet statement, not the protest that she knew it should have been.

He stepped closer to her. "I don't care about the sales deal. Call me at the office later, whenever you're ready for that." His words were heavy with wistfulness. "I was hoping that your unexpected appearance at my apartment meant that you really wanted to see me again."

"Does that really matter to you?" She spoke it as a plea, rather than a question.

"It seems to be the only thing that does matter to me anymore."

In less than a heartbeat, they were locked in each other's arms, holding onto one another with a fierceness that threatened to steal their breath away.

"Sure you don't want to have me arrested for trespassing?" His ragged query teased her ear.

"I might have you arrested if you don't trespass further." The threat emerged as a weak sigh.

He required no additional invitation. His mouth claimed possession of hers with a mastery that promised tenderness, his tongue probing, darting, caressing gently.

A wild sensation, a longing like she'd never before felt, surged through her, and she sensed the same unbridled turbulence coursing through him. They clutched at each other greedily, their kisses harder, driven by a passion to possess and please.

It seemed as if a torrid tempest swirled onto Sunrise Key, enveloping them in another time. They were almost two other people — the only two people in existence.

Chad's mouth descended hungrily on hers again. He kneaded her hips, holding her tightly against him. She could feel the heat created by their close contact, the warm flush that crept over her thighs.

"I've wanted you so much. I haven't thought of anything else," Chad said huskily.

She was too breathless to speak at all. He drew away from her only long enough to slip his hand beneath her full skirt, and slide his palm along the sensitive flesh that eagerly parted to make way for him.

"I want you, too," she gasped, and leaned against him, compressed in his tight embrace.

Their passion swiftly overtook them and they came together as one. As the ocean's waves crashed onto the shore, their desire exploded in a rush of love and fulfillment.

Much later, they walked back to her cottage, arms locked around each other. Chad dropped a kiss on her head. "I never thought of myself as the outdoor type."

"Me either." She gave him a sly smile. "I think we're both quick learners, but I don't think that's exactly a conventional survival technique."

"We do learn quickly together. And that was very necessary to my survival."

Still later, after an extended sojourn in her bed, divested of all their clothes, she traced his face with her fingertip. "I never did find out why you were here so early this morning."

"I couldn't sleep. I wanted to see if you'd have breakfast with me. I guess I wanted to be close to you, imagining you waking up. I was going to sit on the beach alone and watch the sunrise." He grinned. "I liked the unplanned activity better, though."

His hand began a slow journey to the curve of her waistline. "Let's play hookey. Let's have twenty-four hours all for us, no business, no outside world at all."

"That would make it dawn tomorrow."

"Till dawn," he said, pressing his mouth to hers.

Every detail of that day would remain well-defined in her memory forever, no matter what happened in the future.

They spent a lazy day divided between the wildlife preserve, the beach, and the bedroom. For dinner, she wore the one evening dress she'd brought from Boston, an emerald-green silk, joining Chad in the cabin cruiser to Captiva, where they dined at one of the finest restaurants facing the ocean.

Chapter 9

They returned to Sunrise Key after dinner. As they disembarked from the cabin cruiser, Chad said, "Maybe we should have a few dances in the Sunset Ballroom."

"I did ask Jacques to clear away the debris and clean it up. It's not ready for an Inaugural Ball yet, but it would be all ours." No sooner had she said that than she remembered Chad's pensive expression and words the first time they'd toured it with Wick. "Or would it be all ours?" she couldn't help asking. "I had a feeling maybe you had some special memories there with someone else."

His smile slipped away, leaving a ghost in its place. "Your quick mind is one of the things that attracts me to you, but you don't have to be quite that perceptive." He put his arm around her shoulders and gave her a squeeze. "From now on, there's no room in my memories for anyone but you."

He brought a lantern from the boat to light their way along the dark path. They weren't as far as the end of the dock before Denyse could no longer stifle the questions ricocheting through her mind. "Was that very long ago?" Her attempt at a casual lilt wasn't successful.

"Several years."

Good, so far.

"Were you in love with her?" she asked softly.

"Very much."

Whoops. One question too many. She burned to know, and yet it hurt, irrational as that was. "Mind if I ask what happened?"

He drew in a long breath before exhaling a difficult answer. "She chose to marry another man."

Even now, pain was evident in his words. Denyse wouldn't question him further.

She didn't have to. He added voluntarily, gazing across the black ocean, "She said she chose the one who needed her the most. That was kind of ironic since I'd tried all along to be self-sufficient, the kind of man who everyone could depend on."

Denyse rested her hand on his lower arm in a comforting gesture.

"The man was a former fiancé of hers. They'd been parted because —" He hesitated, picking his words. "Due to circumstances beyond their control. I think she loved us both, but she chose him because he needed her more, because he'd suffered —" He stopped himself in mid-sentence.

"And you've been the one suffering ever

since," she observed softly.

"Yes." He added cryptically, "More than you know."

Denyse's insides twisted. Did that mean no one could ever really replace his earlier love?

"Not as much lately," Chad continued. "Time doesn't cure all, but it does take the edge off things." He stopped walking, turned toward her, and pulled her into his arms. "Especially now that I have you." His eyes searched hers. "I do have you, don't I?"

"Yes." It was true and there was no point in denying it or postponing that admission — to him or to herself. She realized now why he'd been so concerned at first about whether she was romantically attracted to Wick. He didn't want the risk of losing another woman if he let himself fall in love again.

"I gather there hasn't been a serious romantic involvement in your life for a while?" His inflection made that a plea for confirmation rather than an observation.

"That's right." She was glad to assure him. "I cared for one man enough for us to try living together for a while, but neither of us was one-hundred percent in love." She recognized that even more now that she'd encountered the all-consuming fire of the love she had found with Chad. She added, "That relationship wasn't meant to last." She told him a little more about Bob Farrell, more than he'd volunteered about his last meaningful liaison.

She didn't want to share him in any way with his past. "Let's make our own ballroom," she suggested. "Let's have our dances on the beach with real starlight glittering above us and the lullaby of the waves as background music." She hastened to add, "Not the shelly beach. The other one."

He agreed with her on the advantages of a Beach Ball. "I'll get a couple of blankets off the boat in case we decide to sit one out."

He sprinted back the length of the pier and returned to her side in no time.

She paused to take off her shoes at the edge of the sand. "Oh, you didn't mention it was a sock hop," he said, jokingly. He hunkered down to assist her and she leaned on his shoulder for support, lifting one foot, then the other.

"You're going to feel really gritty if you try sand dancing in pantyhose," he pointed out from his low vantage point. He insisted on helping her remove those also, slowly slithering the sheer fabric downward, his palms following, setting Denyse on fire.

She wriggled her bare toes into the sand

which was still heated from the sun's caress as she was still heated from Chad's. "One good turn deserves another." She knelt in front of him, untying his shoes, slipping them off, lightly scraping a fingernail along the sole of one foot. The socks came next, and she eased them downward, running her fingertips along his ankles.

Through a medley of selections on the cassette player, they two-stepped, cha-chaed, swirled through swing, and discoed in ways that would have horrified everyone from Arthur Murray to Michael Jackson. In the shifting sand, they spent more time falling against each other and laughing than actually moving their feet.

As Chad popped in a fresh cassette he said, "Last dance." The strains of Strauss echoed across a century. He bowed low before her, then swept her into his arms and across the beach in an attempted waltz rendered hilarious by the treacherous sands.

He swirled her onto the ocean's edge where the incoming velvet waves decorated her ankles with bracelets of lacy foam. She imagined that the waves, too, were waltzing.

Strauss had never fancied an ending to his waltz like the one composed by Chad. His rhythms were as varied as the tempos to which they'd laughingly danced earlier, and transported them in harmonious rapture to those glittering stars and beyond.

Much later, they roused themselves off the beach blanket, opting for the night-long comfort of Denyse's bed. They headed back to the cottage and fell onto the pillows.

"If I stick to our twenty-four-hour agreement for hookey, I have to be up at dawn," Chad muttered drowsily, snuggling her into his arms. "Sounds like an execution."

"Are you begging for a stay of execution?"

"I'm begging to stay — at least a couple of extra hours. Unfortunately, I do have to leave early in the morning for another commitment."

A business appointment on Saturday morning? She supposed that was likely in the real estate business. Maybe it was a power breakfast.

"We could go to the wildlife preserve around sunrise," he was saying. "There is some truth in the old adage about early birds. Our feathered neighbors are on view then."

She hadn't been back to the swamp again since her accident. Going with Chad would be a good way of dispelling her qualms, and she would enjoy watching the birds. "Okay, you have a two-hour reprieve."

"I seem to have worn myself out," he

commented with a chuckle. "I think I'd better set the alarm."

He set the dials and they fell asleep nestled together.

Denyse woke before the alarm demanded it. The dove-colored dawn was seeping through the windows. She delighted in watching Chad sleep. He looked so lovable, so vulnerable. So innocent.

The thought jerked her into the chill light of morning. She still didn't know if Chad was involved in whatever activities her father and/or Wick had been planning. Or whether he was in cahoots with Burt. She couldn't believe he'd been involved in any wrongdoing, but she wouldn't be the first woman who'd lost her judgment when passion intervened.

She started at the sound of the radio announcer, and the voice of one of her favorite vocalists sang out a new tune that seemed as if it were just for her:

> *Close to sunrise, how this one cries,*
> *That the two of us soon must part.*
> *When the dawn wakes, how my soul*
> *   breaks,*
> *Must love end when this day must start.*
> *   If I let go, will I get no,*
> *   Future love from you,*

Oh, we croon sighs, till the moon dies,
But along with it dies my heart.

She tightened her arm around Chad, who was beginning to stir.

Is it unwise, close to sunrise,
To keep clasping you close to me.
Are we gun-shy, though we've spun high,
Is desire now just to flee.
 If I hold on, Will you get sold on,
  Staying in my arms
Till the full moon, or till next June,
till our tenth anniversary.

Chad turned over, wrapping his arm around her. "Morning, beautiful," he murmured. "I love —"

Her heart stopped for an instant.

"— waking up next to you."

"Me, too." She whispered those two words, too inadequate for how she felt now. The radio continued to taunt her.

Have you spun lies, close to sunrise,
That will fade in bright light of day.
When the sun shines, are they just lines,
Like you, will they speed away.
 Why must you go, why don't I know
 How you really feel

163

Close to sunset, how can one get
You to come back to me to stay.

The lyrics lingered in her mind even after
she and Chad were dressed and at the wildlife preserve. The need for maintaining silence in order to enjoy it to the fullest
stilled her from asking him questions.
That, and the fact that she wanted to bask
in the feel of his arms around her and pre-
tend for a while longer that there were no
questions to ask.

They were standing in dappled shadows
beneath trees near the pond. Denyse was
wrapped in Chad's arms, her back against
his chest, his face nestled in her hair.

He pointed up above them, and Denyse
followed his gesture, seeing a cluster of bro-
meliads the color of morning — palest
yellow edged in gold. He quietly raised himself on his tiptoes, stretching to pluck one,
then anchored it behind her ear.

Herons soared above, white wings spread
in graceful flight. An anhinga swooped into
the water, captured breakfast, then perched
on a stump, half-opening its swarthy black
wings to dry. A duck paddled by, followed
by half a dozen babies. Gulls wheeled overhead. A pelican watched it all from a fallen
log on the opposite side of the pond.

Chad lifted his arm in slow motion, unobtrusively directing Denyse's attention. Again, he shared with her something her untrained eyes might never have spotted.

A tiny Key deer emerged warily from amid the foliage, lapping its morning drink from the pond. Chad had explained that these deer, tailored in miniature by Nature as if to fit the teensy islands they inhabited, were indigenous to the Florida Keys. Only relatively small numbers of the deer had survived into this decade, and Dennis had had a few transported here where they could be safe and perpetuate the species. They tended to be shy, rarely seen.

Denyse and Chad remained in silent communion with each other as well as with nature for more than an hour. When Chad moved away, indicating time to go, they strolled back slowly with arms around each other, not speaking until they reached the earthen dike.

"That was beautiful," she told him unnecessarily. "You have some of the best ideas. Now, what would you like for breakfast? Not fish, too, I hope."

"Sorry, I don't have time for breakfast. Like I mentioned, I have to be someplace else early this morning." A smile slid across his handsome features. "About

165

those best ideas, though . . ."

"Yes?"

"Let's do our twenty-four-hour time warp every week from now on, only turn it into two days plus. No matter what you're doing with regard to selling or running Sunrise Key, no matter what my business demands are, let's be like average people. Let's quit working, discussing business, or thinking about work at six P.M. every Friday night, and not start business again until six A.M. on Monday morning."

"A weekly truce?" She returned his smile.

"I didn't know we were adversaries."

She relented. "A weekly time warp, then." She didn't need much encouragement. Still, she pointed out, "But there's so much work to be done here, and apparently you normally work on the weekends."

"Everything will get done eventually, sooner or later. And we'll have part of every week for us, no matter what. It doesn't even have to be your place or mine. I could rent us a hideaway up or down the coast where we could be alone." He paused. "Are you tempted?"

"Very."

"You haven't seen the area yet. We can play tourist if you want to. Thomas Edison's winter home is in Fort Myers, with a museum and a botanical garden of exotic trees and plants from all over the world that he brought for experimentation. As for other possible local alternatives," he pondered for a minute, "I could take you over to Lehigh Acres and show you the library where the whistle-blowing secret agent, John what's-his-name, held his national press conference not long ago."

"That's becoming more resistible."

"Whoops. Well, if you want to see some swamps besides your own, we can go to the Everglades or Corkscrew Sanctuary." He expanded the scope of his sales pitch. "We can safari through the outdoor zoo at Busch Gardens in Tampa, or watch water skiers at Cypress Gardens. Even go to Epcot Center and Disney World."

She laughed. "How can I possibly say no to a man who offers me Mickey Mouse? I'll pencil you in for the next few weekends."

"Ink me in. And get an expanded calendar." He drew her into his arms.

The cadence of her pulse accelerated, whether from his touch or from his words, she couldn't tell. "Seriously, darling, I like the personal tours you've conducted very much so far. I think that same itinerary will be all we'll need in the immediate future."

He signaled his agreement with a deep kiss.

She walked with him to the cabin cruiser. "So are we starting with the rest of this weekend?" she asked eagerly. "What time will you be back from your appointment?"

"Sorry, honey." He looked away from her. "My whole weekend's committed. But we'll start at six P.M. next Friday."

Unless I sell to your clients in the meantime, she realized. That would bring our business to a rapid conclusion that might mean we could be together seven days a week. But she was leaning toward operating the resort rather than selling if she could possibly manage the necessary financial maneuverings to do that.

What would happen to her relationship with Chad if she didn't sell at all or sold to other buyers?

She couldn't help wondering. As he sailed away, her confidence sailed with him and all the former doubts and insecurities washed back in force.

Was he meeting Wick? At least then he wouldn't be with another woman.

Wick was shipping himself off somewhere this Saturday morning, too. She'd overheard Carlos mention that to Consuela in the kitchen the other day, and the fact that the conversation had halted abruptly when they had noticed her made her wonder what Wick was up to.

She remembered Wick's reaction when she'd said she'd be keeping an eye on things. Had Chad's unexpected appearance here yesterday been designed to divert her attention from other matters? He'd succeeded in that.

Suddenly, she wondered if Burt really was taking the vacation she'd tried to manipulate him into taking. Maybe Burt was a third party to the plot she still hadn't figured out.

Chapter 10

She fixed her own early breakfast. She would have to speak to Consuela and Carlos about the waste of food. Apparently no one stopped the stock orders even when the resort had no guests. There was no way that supply of food could be consumed by four people, and they must have thrown out much of the earlier inventory that would have spoiled by now. She'd have to hire an experienced food service manager soon, or see if there was an independent purchasing service she could retain. Despite Consuela's culinary skills, she obviously understood nothing about cost effectiveness and supply exceeding demand.

Nervous energy drove her. She forced herself to wait until a decent hour before telephoning Burt with a fabricated question to see if he was home.

There was no answer.

She called Chad's business number and his answering service said he wouldn't be available until Monday. An answering machine with the usual, vague hope-you're-not-a-burglar message picked up his home line.

She wished she knew how to raise Wick

on the radiophone, although she hadn't an inkling what she'd say to him anyway. "Hi, just called to see if you were doing something illegal this weekend? And by the way, are Chad and Burt with you?"

It was possible, of course, that Burt had left town for his vacation, that there was nothing to her foreboding.

Still, she had Carlos take her to Captiva, then drove the resort's car to Chad and Burt's condo building. To check, she leaned on Chad's doorbell for several minutes. There was no response.

There was a similar lack of response at Burt's front door. An elderly lady was returning along the outdoor corridor with mail in hand. "May I help you?" she asked.

Don't tell me Burt stole all that money for operations for his poor old gray-haired mother, Denyse thought. He didn't seem the type. "You live here?" she asked, incredulous.

"Next door. But if you're looking for Mr. Johnson, I think he's gone out of town for a while. When I was bringing in my newspaper about an hour ago, I saw him leaving with several suitcases. I asked if he wanted me to water his plants or anything, but he said it wouldn't matter if they died." Indignation flared on her kind face. "Imagine owning a living thing and not taking care of it!"

"That's awful. As his employer, I'll speak to him about bringing his plants to the office where we can water them when he's out of town."

It had apparently not occurred to the neighbor that Denyse might be a potential burglar, but she softened further in view of her sympathetic approach to potted foliage.

"You didn't happen to notice," Denyse questioned, "whether Mr. Chadwick from number 211 was with him?"

"Oh, no. However, when I was taking in the milk, I did see Mr. Chadwick leaving in his blue jeans with some sort of duffel bag." She pondered for an additional moment. "I don't believe I've ever seen the two of them together."

"One more thing, if you don't mind, please," Denyse said. "I promised Mr. Johnson I'd take care of some maintenance on his car as soon as I had a chance, since he's used it some for business. But I'm not sure which car in the parking garage is his."

"Why it's the red Corvette. I saw it there when I went down for my mail. Guess he didn't drive today."

"He probably intended to leave it here for me," Denyse said with stabs of remorse for lying to the friendly but naive woman. She chatted politely for a few more minutes, eager to make her own getaway.

So Burt had left this morning, too, with a means of transportation other than his own car. But she couldn't call the police and ask them to close the bus, train, and airport terminals and "stop that man." She hadn't filed a formal criminal complaint yet.

Besides, she realized, the greater likelihood was that Burt was on Wick's boat, although he could be on another boat or riding in someone else's car. The parking garage revealed that Chad's car was there, too.

Of the other three choices, though, given Burt's expensive tastes, she surmised that he would opt for the airport, probably first class. Uncertain what was compelling her onward, she made the long drive there.

She saw that five flights had departed within the past hour, but gambled on the silver jet now taking off. Despite Burt's lousy behavior otherwise, she had never known him to be late, so he probably had checked in an hour early for his flight. According to the board, its destination was Miami.

"Darn," she said breathlessly to the customer service agent, "I was trying to catch my office manager, Burt Johnson, before that plane took off. He left behind some important papers that he's going to need for a meeting. I'll have to FAX them to a messenger service and have them delivered to the airport at his destination. Can you tell me what time that flight will land?"

The woman punched a few keys on her computer. "Burt Johnson is on that flight, but you'd be cutting it pretty close to have anything delivered to him at the Miami airport. The flight takes less than an hour." She stared at the screen for a moment. "Oh, I guess you meant you wanted to send them to his final destination, since he's connecting to a Rio flight."

"Rio de Janeiro, Brazil." Denyse attempted to make that sound like a confirmation and not like the expression of surprise that it really was.

The customer service agent gave her the flight's arrival time.

No sense calling Brazil, Denyse knew. There was no extradition from Brazil.

There was a slim possibility that Burt had gone for a vacation and would be back. Maybe a major foreign trip for only four days was within the champagne budget of an embezzler. But she doubted it.

Burt had fled to avoid criminal prosecution. And that meant that either Wick had warned him or that Wick had told his brother and Chad had tipped off Burt.

Maybe they were all on their way to Brazil together. There were more layers for her to uncover; she'd always known that.

A call from the pay phone to the connecting airline to confirm reservations in the last name of Chadwick revealed that there were no such reservations. But that didn't mean Chad and Wick weren't on different flights or sailing Wick's boat toward *The Girl From Ipanema.*

She returned to her office and tried to busy herself until evening when she joined Carlos, Consuela, and Jacques for dinner, again unintentionally causing an abrupt pause in the conversation.

After dinner, she remarked casually, "Maybe we should have a barbecue when Wick gets back."

"He did not tell you?" Carlos said, surprised.

Denyse suspected the twitch that followed resulted from a jab in the ribs by Consuela.

"We will do the bee-bar-kay," Consuela interjected swiftly, stumbling over the unfamiliar syllables, "if you will show me how."

"It just sort of means cooking outdoors."

Consuela looked puzzled. "But America means indoor everything."

"A regular dinner to celebrate his return will be all right."

Consuela hesitated, apparently due to uncertainty as to how much Denyse really knew. "*Bien.* Will I ask Señor Wick on Monday what menu he wants?"

"That's fine."

Was Wick really coming back on Monday? Or had these other three employees been involved also, and had not been clued in to join in the getaway? Or were they just covering for Wick? Or tricked by Wick and/or Chad and completely unaware of the escape?

She paused on the way back to her own cottage to have a one-sided chat with Clayton. Carlos and Jacques had fashioned a chain-link pen, fancier than the original, with greater square footage than some people's houses. A natural pond, little more than an oversized puddle, was at one edge.

"Clayton, you're the only one in a thousand-mile radius who I can really trust." She proceeded to review the situation with him, as if speaking aloud and listening to the unsolved riddles would miraculously provide clues. He paid attention politely for a while, then shifted his interest to the tidbit of food he was rolling back and forth in his tiny front paws. She finished with, "For the answers to these and other burning questions, tune in on Monday."

Clayton popped the food into his mouth.

She continued to her cottage, still muttering aloud. "Good grief, Denyse. Now you're discussing business with a raccoon. The real estate syndicate can probably take over the island by having you committed to an institution." Then she realized that, even worse than talking to a raccoon, she was talking aloud to herself.

That night, she initiated casual, but lengthy and chatty long-distance calls to her mother, her stepfather, Kelly, and a college friend she hadn't talked to in six months. She didn't review her problems with anyone except Kelly, but she was determined to participate in some conversations which were two-way and where she didn't have to search for hidden nuances in every remark.

Her next communication was with her father, Dennis Benton.

He didn't pay her a ghostly visit, but she discovered that part of her legacy was the truth, with an insight into her father's character.

Rummaging through boxes in his closet,

she found that most of the boxes contained her. Her baby pictures, along with photos of her mother, and the three of them together. School pictures of her for each year. Pictures of her at every birthday party.

She remembered her maternal grandparents had upheld a tradition of snapping photos on every birthday, even when she'd been an upstart adolescent protesting such plebian activities. Now she understood where some of the pictures had wound up.

There were other mementos, too: photos at Christmases as well as other holidays and special occasions. Her high school and college graduation announcements.

Had he waited, she wondered, for her wedding announcement, for announcements of grandchildren?

Unchecked tears trickled down her cheeks as she read the letters on fine stationery, accumulated by her father over a quarter of a century. Her grandfather had written dutiful, quarterly reports as if she were some sort of corporation.

From the earliest letters, she pieced together the fact that when her parents had divorced, her grandparents had convinced Dennis that it was best for his child if she had no contact with him rather than having to become accustomed to a largely absentee father. For the first year or so, Dennis had defied that, still insisting on visitation rights with Denyse although she was too young to remember seeing him. But after her mother had become engaged to remarry, Dennis had relented and agreed to sever all direct contact with Denyse as long as her grandparents kept him up to date with her progress and problems. He, too, had decided it was best if a young child knew only one father.

Her mother had refused child support, since the family was financially comfortable, according to one of her grandfather's letters. Not much reading between the lines was necessary to comprehend that her mother didn't want monthly reminders of her father, that she needed a permanent unbinding of those ties if her next marriage was to work.

At the top of one box were ribbon-tied bundles of well-worn letters from her mother to Dennis during their courtship and brief marriage. Apparently he'd reread them often.

Eventually, with her cheeks still dewy, Denyse curled into bed, grateful that she knew and understood her father a little better.

Her original purpose in looking through the stored boxes was postponed.

She tried to work in her office on Sunday, but accomplished little as her mind wandered everywhere except to the papers on her desk.

Late Sunday afternoon, with a twinge in her heart, she resumed her search of Dennis's closet for her original goal — finding a gun if he'd had one.

She figured if Wick was due back Monday he'd be docking before daybreak, and she intended to conduct a private surveillance of the narrow beach on the opposite side of the island where he had said he most often anchored. Dread seeped through her, and she couldn't separate how much was fear of what she would learn and how much was apprehension at remaining alone all night at the edge of the swamp.

But she would do this, because she needed to know what Wick unloaded from his boat when he anchored, and who was involved with him. She prayed it wouldn't be Chad.

She doubted that she could fire a gun at Wick, much less at Chad, but she tried to convince herself that if it was necessary for self-defense she would. However, no weapon handily revealed itself. She considered taking a butcher knife from the kitchen, but was wary of falling on that herself.

Her best defense would be silence. She intended only to observe from some concealed position, not to confront anyone no matter what.

A perverse fragment of her subconscious hoped that Chad and Wick had both made a final getaway if they had been doing something illegal. Although that meant she would never be in Chad's arms again, at least it wouldn't be she who directly delivered him to the arms of the law.

She took a sweater and a sweatshirt in case the night grew cold; it seemed an iciness was spreading from within her already. Along with a blanket, binoculars, and a supply of food and coffee, she set out. She also took her camera in case she could force herself to document whatever happened.

As she started out, the afternoon sun was still bright enough to chase away every sinister shadow from Sunrise Key. Instead of taking the direct path through the swamp, she took the much longer route around the perimeter of the island. Where the shoreline became a tangle of overgrowth, she waded out and went around through the shallow water.

She told herself that it was fear of snakes that compelled her to take the long way around, although she'd learned that water moccasins and other snakes could swim and would as likely be found in the brackish water around the tangled edges of the island as in the interior.

Arriving at the narrow strip of beach on the other side, she selected a spot well-concealed by a low fanning palm and a thicket of other greenery where she could peer through a vantage point without easily being seen.

She was on the sunrise side of the island, so the bright sun's traitorous retreat was a reflection of orange, deepening to streaks of blood red. Then blackness pounced on her, enveloping her.

She endured a night filled with unidentified sounds — leaves rustling, slitherings that were probably more imagined than real.

What if I'm going through this for nothing? she wondered. She hoped nothing turned up, that Wick and Chad would appear and all would be right with the world. Still, the world itself was far from all right.

She'd brought strong coffee to ward off any temptation to sleep, but nervous tension held her as tightly upright as if steel wires had been threaded through her. The night was the longest she'd ever spent.

Finally, dawn yawned over the horizon.

She blinked her eyes, staring into the ashen light.

Yes, it was there.

From the mouth of dawn, a large boat emerged, its neutral gray color camouflaging it in the start of day.

Denyse watched, almost forgetting to breathe, as the boat progressed toward her, seeming to point straight at her accusingly.

Chapter 11

Minutes plodded past while the boat slowed near shore and an anchor clanged its way downward to bite into the sand. Denyse was shocked to see the boat's sides punctured and splintered by gunfire.

Then a small boat containing one man was lowered, and he rowed the short distance to shore. He quickly scouted the length of the beach, a ways along the path inland, then back toward the direction where Denyse waited. She raised the binoculars to check one more time. Soon the man was close enough that binoculars weren't necessary.

There was no doubt of the identification.

The boat was definitely Wick's, despite the new decor of bullet holes and the heavy machine guns that must have been disguised before but were now visible above the decks.

The advance man on the shore was Chad.

Her heart burrowed into the sand beneath her, burying her most treasured memories with it.

"Everything looks okay," Chad yelled toward the boat, waving his arms in the air.

Then his gaze was pulled straight in her direction, as if magnetized. "Hey, look over there." He pointed at her.

She didn't know how he'd spotted her, but she popped out of her not-so-concealed position, turning to run.

"Denyse!" Chad yelled.

Only then did she see a short distance behind her, parallel with her position, a small herd of the rare Key deer. That's what he'd been pointing out to Wick.

At all the noise and movement, the deer skittered away, vanishing in an instant. She intended to do the same.

She set out at a run, away from the boat. But the heavy sand dragged at her feet, shifted beneath her, hampered every step.

"Denyse, wait!" Chad was calling behind her. His voice grew closer each time. "Why are you running from me?"

A lasso of flesh tightened around her. Chad captured her in his arms, but she continued to struggle, trying to stomp on his foot and kick him anywhere she could.

Mostly, he skillfully evaded her flailing legs and arms and finally secured her limbs under his. "What are you doing here? Why are you fighting me?" His questions emerged amid ughs and grunts as she wriggled against him.

"Let go of me!" she ground out between puffs of breath. "Let me go. I sent letters to people with my suspicions," she lied, wishing she'd thought of that. But she hadn't expected to be seen. "If anything happens to me, they'll know you did it. You'll never get away —"

He released her so quickly that she lost her balance, falling onto the thick sand, catching herself with her arms and flipping herself into a sitting position with an *oomph* that marked the departure of all her breath.

"You think I'd hurt you?" His question was a raw wound.

Chad dropped to his knees in the sand beside her, careful not to touch her. "How could you think I'd hurt you?" he repeated, incredulity mingled with tenderness on his features. "*Why* would I?"

"To cover up your . . . activities."

"You thought I'd hurt you?" The topaz eyes opened even wider. "Even kill you — or anybody?"

Her own gaze at the boat provided his answer.

"Denyse, you don't think I'd do anything bad criminal?"

"Bad criminal? Isn't that redundant?"

He looked away from her, his eyes drilling into the sand. "Not necessarily."

"There's such a thing as good criminal?"

"Maybe," he mumbled. "I've wondered that for years and never really answered it myself."

"Good criminals don't have to fight off the Coast Guard," she said, annoyed at the wrench within her that Chad might have been injured.

"Coast Guard?" He didn't understand.

She gestured toward the splintered side of the boat.

"Don't tell me you guys did the new decor yourselves just to enhance the macho image."

"It wasn't the Coast Guard," he responded, astonished. "It was pirates."

"Oh sure. Captain Kidd and Blackbeard happened to materialize. Was this anywhere in the vicinity of the Bermuda Triangle?"

"There are plenty of modern pirates plying the Caribbean, Denyse. Drug runners who take over small defenseless boats to use in their trade, often killing everyone on board."

"How nice that you've only been involved in drug wars instead of skirmishing with the Coast Guard," she commented venomously.

"Another boat attacked us," he pointed out. "We defended ourselves. Successfully, although you don't seem too happy about that."

"Unhappy is a pretty weak word for how I feel right now," she mumbled.

"If finding out this about me means you don't want to be with me anymore" — his words were etched in the deepest tones of disappointment — "then I guess we really weren't meant to be together."

"You've got to be kidding. How could you ever assume that I'd put up with something like this?"

He stared at her. "I have mixed feelings about what we're doing, but at least I see the good in it. You're not the woman I thought you were if you can't see at least a glimmer of good in this."

"Good? You're not only kidding me, you're kidding yourself if you think any good could possibly come from this. You *must* have had your brains scrambled in the Bermuda Triangle."

Comprehension eased into his expression. "Wait a minute. Are we talking about the same —" He hesitated, adopting a poker face. "You're planning to turn me in, aren't you?"

Yes, she was going to turn him in. But she wasn't stupid enough to admit that here with Wick coming off the boat toward them. Yet, even now, gazing into those eyes from which she'd imagined his love flowing, she couldn't lie to him.

"You said you'd never kill anybody," she reminded him weakly.

"That's true."

"Chad," the words were torn from her, "drugs kill."

"And for that, you *would* turn me in?"

A giant-sized lump in her throat prevented her from lying to protect herself, although she did intend to turn him in. She looked away, and a mist of tears veiled her view.

"Good for you," he said in a tone of hearty congratulations. "You are my kind of woman, if you'd send me to jail."

"What? You want to go where the pinstripes are wider?"

"Nope." His voice was downright jaunty now. "But I have a feeling you plan to report me as a drug smuggler. Which is exactly what you should do, if I were involved in anything so vile."

Relief lit her features. "You're not running drugs?"

"Absolutely not. Search all you want."

"Then what —"

Wick reached them then from his jog up the beach. He directed angry words not at Denyse, but at Chad. "I can't believe you told her! Even after all our arguments about telling her right away, you promised you'd wait until after this last run, until after everyone was safe!"

"I didn't tell her. She guessed something was up and staked us out. Since you're the one who insisted on not telling her, you may be interested in knowing that she was planning on turning us in for drug smuggling."

"Drugs? Us?" Wick was righteously astonished. When he recovered, he said to Denyse, "I guess Chad was right. He wanted to tell you and I talked him out of it."

"Tell me what?" she practically screamed at them. "What's on that boat?"

"It's our version of People Express," Chad answered. "Dennis called it Oppressed Express. We bring political refugees here from other countries and try and help them start new lives."

For once, Denyse was speechless.

Chad continued. "Dennis found a new mission in life in his last few years. Sunrise Key has been a way station for immigrants in search of new tomorrows."

"Illegals," Denyse realized aloud, not making any judgment.

"Yes, but we try and help most of them apply for legal amnesty. Everyone deserves a chance at a good, peaceful life and we believe in freedom enough to risk our own lives while securing it for others."

"Exactly how do you wind up with a job like this?" she asked.

"It started several years ago," Chad began. "Ramon Tomas, my business partner, had escaped from Cuba, along with his sister, Lola. They never stopped hoping to engineer the escape of relatives and friends."

Chad went on to explain that he'd had a number of contacts, not only with Latino leaders in southern Florida, but with people of power and wealth in Caribbean and Latin American countries who were investing their often-ill-gotten gains in real estate. When travel restrictions to Cuba eased a bit, Chad had gone there on the pretext of business, actually setting up escape plans for the Tomas's relatives and friends.

"I had expected to do this only one time," he said. "But with each boatload, there were more relatives, more friends, to be rescued from the tragedy that is Cuba. Dennis and Wick caught the fever, intending to go on with these operations even without my continued involvement."

It took over half an hour for the story to be outlined, longer than would have been necessary if Wick hadn't kept interrupting to add his comments. Denyse extracted from the conversational exchanges between the two brothers — sometimes heated and resentful, sometimes admiring and supportive — as much as she learned from their narratives.

"Consuela and Carlos are Cubans," Chad explained. "Dennis has employed them since our second run. Jacques came from Haiti a little later. He was active in the opposition to Duvalier. Even now he might be murdered if he was found. That's why he rarely leaves the island, and why he panicked the night he mistakenly interrupted our speaking of Tonto for *Tontons,* the nickname for the *Tonton Macoute,* the terrorizing secret police of Haiti. Jacques, Consuela, and Carlos have all taken advantage of immigration amnesty to become U.S. citizens."

"At least those three are safe from Burt now," Wick said. "But a lot of other people might not be, so we have to talk about turning him in, Denyse."

"So Burt was involved in this, too?"

"In a backward way," Wick answered. "He was a laggard who used to fish a lot from a small motorboat in these waters. He caught on and used the threat of exposure to blackmail Dennis into giving him a job. He could have exposed not only the three of us, but also many of the people we'd helped. That could have been a death sentence for some of them, like Jacques, if they were caught and deported."

"Then, by embezzling the resort's funds, he continued blackmailing my father." Using the word father and thinking of Dennis at the same time gave Denyse an emotional start, but not an unpleasant one.

"Dennis knew Burt was doing that," Wick said. "But it bought Burt's continued silence."

"If Burt had been a smart blackmailer," Chad pointed out, "he wouldn't have done something that could so obviously condemn him as a criminal."

"So is that why you two warned him, to keep him shut up?"

"Warned him?" the brothers said in unison. They claimed they didn't know what she was talking about.

She decided to wait to see whether Burt appeared at his desk on Wednesday morning before outright accusing Wick of violating his promise.

Chad explained, "Burt's embezzlement was only one of the factors in Sunrise Key's financial decline. Dennis turned down guest reservations for certain periods of the year so the other operations could take place without risk of being observed. He was trying to strike a balance between making enough money to retain the island, and making it available to — shall we say — nonpaying guests."

"That's why the kitchen is so well stocked," Denyse realized. "And why the food disappears." She looked at Wick. "You brought a boatload of people that first day we met, because you didn't know Dennis had died."

"Right. And because we couldn't take a chance on how you'd react, we housed them temporarily in that cinderblock storage building halfway into the swamp, which we've used at other times when people had to be totally under wraps." Wick expelled a breath as if there was something more to tell her, but he didn't want to.

Chad intervened. "A family of half a dozen from El Salvador was there the day you sought shelter from the rain. They didn't know who you were, and a thirteen-year-old panicked and hit you —"

Wick interrupted. "You have to re-member, Denyse, that an expected visitor could be from a death squad in El Salvador. She didn't know better —"

"It was a girl?"

"Yes, a girl who thought she was protecting her family. But the father came and got me right away."

"I'm sorry," Chad said.

"Sorry wasn't the word for it," Wick commented. "Chad raised a considerable ruckus, especially since he'd wanted to tell you all along. It was me who swore you weren't the type to go poking around in the swamp alone."

"Not the type of babe," she mumbled wryly.

"What?"

"Never mind. Go on." She prodded, "You said the last people were from El Salvador. Isn't that a long boat trip from here?"

"Yes and no," Wick answered. "I could go all the way with my boat, but I don't. I pick up the people from Central America at a small islet near Jamaica. It's a way station, too, in an ocean-going underground railroad."

"We pick our times carefully," Chad said. "Never run on a predictable schedule, log things several weeks, even several months apart."

"We took advantage of the Fourth of July" — Wick's voice became strangely distant — "to bring in extra loads of people because my boat could mingle so easily with all the pleasure craft out that weekend. Dennis worked really hard then, and I guess the strain brought on his heart attack. I shouldn't have let him —"

"You couldn't have stopped him," Chad said, comforting in a matter-of-fact tone. "Dennis was doing exactly what he wanted to do."

"Where is my father buried? I was planning to call the lawyer and ask so I can visit the grave."

"About time," Wick mumbled darkly.

"I'm sorry. I hadn't known him and I hadn't known how he'd felt about me until Saturday night." She told them about the letters she'd found.

"I knew about all that," Chad said.

"You knew? How come Dennis didn't tell me?" Wick asked, obviously hurt at having been excluded from Dennis's confidences.

"I guess I was the one he chose to share it with," Chad responded.

"Oh, sure," Wick appeared to realize aloud, "because of —" He glanced at Denyse. "Well, because."

"To answer your question, Denyse," Chad said, "your father is buried right over there, past the edge of the beach, as he chose."

"I didn't know until after he'd died that

196

Chad had helped him with all the advance arrangements," Wick said. "They went through a lot of rigamarole, having to establish and license a section as an official cemetery."

"That meant Dennis could stay on his island always, no matter what." Chad continued, "He had insisted that he wanted a prompt burial before anyone other than his lawyer and I were notified of his death. He didn't want you to have any worries in that regard, or any other regard, Denyse. Frankly, he didn't expect that you would ever come to the island at all. He assumed you'd stay in Boston and sell it from afar without even seeing it."

"Says you," Wick challenged him with a flare of the old rivalry.

"It's true. You know we were winding down our People Express."

"You'd been wanting to quit for a long time," Wick said accusingly.

"Is that right?" Denyse was curious.

"For a lot of reasons," Chad explained. "I'd like to save those whose lives are in danger. But much of the time, we're helping people who are in no immediate danger but want a better life. Despite how noble that sounds, I worry about how happy they are ultimately, transplanted into a totally foreign environment, prey to unscrupulous employers who exploit them. Dennis couldn't employ any more than Consuela, Carlos, and Jacques here. It might have called too much attention to the place. We take no payment for what we do, but sometimes we wind up working through sleazy middlemen who've demanded whatever little money these people may have. I never agreed with that, nor with too many unnecessary risks."

A lively discussion between Chad and Wick ensued, obviously not for the first time. The gist was that Chad believed that Wick took too many hot-dog chances, jeopardizing not only himself but others.

Chad picked up the thread of narrative again. "I've always felt that the longer we continue, the more we tempt fate."

"Like this trip? The pirate attack?" Denyse asked softly.

"At least we were prepared for this one," Wick said.

"For this one? Have there been others?"

"The first was several months ago. New Year's fireworks. The boat wasn't fortified then, and the attack was sudden and unexpected." Chad's voice drifted, then resumed. "A few people died in that attack, including Porque's parents. I can't help but feel that they would have been better off staying in Cuba."

"I hope Porque wasn't on board this time —"

"You can't think I'd put the kid at the risk of that again," Wick responded, miffed at her question. "He stays with Consuela and Carlos whenever I'm on a run."

"They've offered to take him permanently," Chad said quietly. "So have I. But he insists on staying with Wick."

"What can I say?" Wick affected a swagger in his voice. "At least one person finds me irresistible." He directed a rakish wink at Denyse, but shining in his eyes was a parental care and sense of belonging definitely incongruent with his swashbuckler image.

"When I mentioned tempting fate," Chad picked up that thread, "I didn't mean only pirate attacks. Sometimes I worry that we've built a house of cards, that if we bring in too many, we put at risk some of the others. Who knows what the domino effect could be. Besides, I'd rather be using my contacts and any limited influence I might have to try for changes that would benefit many people within their own countries rather than just the few we can transport away from the problems. I can't do that and call attention to myself as long as we're doing this."

"It's been a frustration for Chad to stay so much behind the scenes." Wick grudgingly allocated some credit to his brother. "He's given a lot of money anonymously to organizations like Amnesty International and Amigòs — hands-on groups — but he hasn't been able to work with them openly."

The inherent rivalry returned. "Speaking of money," Wick said, "I bet Dennis didn't know that you were going to offer Denyse a million and a half dollars less than you'd offered him."

"I didn't offer it at all. The buyers did. Dennis expected that the offer to his daughter would drop; he knew that seven million was too high. Neither he nor I could know precisely what the buyers would propose for a new seller. He couldn't have known how much longer he had — it could have been weeks or years. He simply wanted to continue his Express as long as possible."

"See, Denyse, he didn't want to sell." Wick seized the opportunity to renew his pleas. "He wanted us to go on as long as possible. Maybe just another year, even a few months . . ."

This time, the interruption came from Chad. "I won't let you involve Denyse." He turned to her. "About the people on the boat today, we had a commitment and no choice. But Wick's already promised — no more after this. And if you want, we can try to hide them at my place in Fort Myers, far away from involving you."

"No. Of course, they can stay, use the guest cottages, while you make whatever are your usual arrangements — although it's probably just as well if I don't know about those." She looked back and forth between the two brothers. "For not having to make a difficult decision on subsequent operations of this type, I owe my thanks, along with millions of dollars, to the IRS. I'm glad that I don't have to wrestle with all the legal and moral issues involved — although I expect I would say that Sunrise Key belonged to my father and should be used however he wished."

She pointed out as she'd already told Wick, "I have inheritance tax due soon. I have no choice but to sell or to make this resort profitable, and it can't be profitable enough to make major payments on a mortgage to cover the inheritance tax with only a part-time operation."

"The people today can stay awhile though?" Wick confirmed.

"There seems to be plenty of food,"

Denyse replied with a twinkle in her eyes.

"I'll start getting them off the boat," Wick said. Not too diplomatically, he added, "Have you told Denyse everything about Lola?"

Chad laughed. "I guess I'd have to now."

"Well, you're the superhonest, upstanding one," Wick countered. "I just wondered — oh, never mind —"

"I was going to tell her anyway."

"Tell me while we walk down to my father's grave," Denyse said.

Wick returned to the boat as they walked, Denyse's arm linked through Chad's, in the opposite direction.

She spoke first. "Lola is your memory from the Sunset Ballroom, isn't she?"

"Yes," he replied hesitantly. "But there's more. Lola's also the mother of my child."

"What?" Denyse halted mid-step.

There was a distant echo of anguish in his words. "I didn't know until after the child, my son, was born and I pieced together the dates. As I told you, Lola had chosen to marry someone else, someone she thought needed her more than I."

"Oh, Chad." She squeezed his arm in sympathy.

"The someone else was a former fiancé.

He'd been imprisoned for a while in Cuba, partly because of his activities in helping Lola and Ramon escape. He was captured at the same time they got away."

"At least he finally escaped, too."

"He was among the first group of people that I — we — got out of Cuba."

Several seconds passed before Chad continued. "About my son, the arrangement is much like Dennis's was. That's probably why he confided in me. They moved to the Midwest, and Lola begged me to relinquish any claim on my child, never see him, allow them to be a family."

He swallowed hard, and Denyse resisted an urge to touch him. "There wasn't anything I could do. Not without tearing the child and Lola apart. Her husband is a very good man. I set up a trust fund for support and education until he's twenty-two, and another to give him a start after that. Otherwise, Ramon passes me pictures and verbal reports about my son."

"Is that why you never wanted another child, because the risk of pain was too great?" Denyse asked softly.

"I didn't think so. But who knows how much the pain played a part in my decision." His eyes searched hers. "You really don't mind not having children?"

"All I'd really mind is not having the man I love."

She embraced him and he joyfully joined his lips to hers.

They resumed their walk. "Speaking of children, is it really best for Porque to be with Wick?"

"Better than it might appear. First of all, being with Wick is what Porque wants; that's his stability. Secondly, Wick is a surprisingly responsible father-type. Porque wasn't ready to start school in a strange country right after his parents were killed, but Wick's been tutoring him in a way. He started by reading him classic comic books, but I think they've worked their way up to modern classics, although I suspect their taste runs to books like *Jaws*."

A few minutes later, Denyse was paying her respects at the graveside of the father she was only starting to know.

Later that afternoon, the last contingent of refugees expressed their gratitude at that same graveside of a benefactor they'd never know. The refugees joined Denyse, Chad, Wick, Porque, Wick's first mate Pablo, Consuela, Carlos, and Jacques for an impromptu memorial service.

Wick delivered an eloquent eulogy.

That made Denyse feel even sorrier that

she had lambasted him earlier that day, after their new guests had been made comfortable, for warning Burt and enabling him to get away. Wick had absolutely denied tipping off Burt, or even telling Chad. Chad claimed that he hadn't been aware until today that Denyse had discovered Burt's embezzlement.

After dinner, alone with Wick and Chad, she apologized profusely to Wick for falsely accusing him. "The bank manager called later in the morning to tell me that Burt had stopped in Friday afternoon to cash a fifty-dollar check, and they'd turned him down. They'd tried to call me then, but I was — incommunicado."

"Is that what they're calling it now?" Chad said with a chuckle, fondly remembering their day together.

"Imagine. For what was almost certainly a legitimate check needed for petty cash at the resort, Burt realized I was on to him and was able to get away."

"You must recognize, though," Chad admitted, "that we're not entirely sorry that Burt eluded you. Much as we'd like to see him punished, he could have hurt a lot of people if he'd told everything he knew, including us."

"I suppose so," she said with a sigh.

"Once I knew the whole story, I probably would have agreed with you and made some sort of deal to fire him and stop his blackmail and embezzlement, but promise not to file criminal charges as long as he kept his mouth shut."

"Maybe it's better that he didn't have time to plan," Chad said. "If he doesn't show up on Wednesday, you can still provide all the evidence to the District Attorney. Burt's personal assets could be frozen. He may have withdrawn all his cash, but he wouldn't have had an opportunity to sell his condo, which is worth about a quarter of a million dollars." He leaned closer, conspiratorially. "And I have it on good authority that Burt paid cash in full. The entire proceeds from the sale of his condo can go to the resort as partial restitution."

"Maybe it is a punishment of sorts," Wick said strangely, "to have to flee your own home for a foreign land. Maybe Burt is being punished, with an ironic twist of justice, for his threats to turn in people who needed sanctuary here."

Not surprisingly, Burt didn't show up or call on Wednesday. Denyse waited a couple more days, until all of the last group of refugees had been dispersed. Chad and Wick had been coming and going, and each time they left, one or two other people disappeared with them. It was best that she didn't know the details.

By Thursday night, the final refugee was settled elsewhere.

Wick didn't return until late. Denyse and Chad were waiting, and dinner was an informal, after-dark cookout for the three of them with a bonfire on the main beach. After the last marshmallow had been stickily consumed, they enjoyed companionable chatting.

"I suppose I should have asked you, Denyse, but I didn't think you'd mind," Wick said. "I planted flowers on Dennis's grave today. Different varieties in shades of yellow, peach, and pink." He added, almost sheepishly, "In the shape of a key."

"So Dennis will always have his Sunrise Key," Denyse recognized.

"No matter what," Wick murmured.

"Of course, it's okay."

"Carlos and Jacques will maintain it, but I wanted to plant it myself before I leave."

"You're leaving?"

"It's best. Much as I tried to hang onto what we'd been doing here as long as I could, the hard fact is that my boat is becoming too well known, too easily recognizable in these waters. I thought I'd check out the Louisiana bayous. Besides, Porque should be in school. I think maybe we'll rent a place in New Orleans. I might even get a real job."

"All you have to do," Denyse teased, "is look in the classifieds under swashbuckler."

They all laughed together, covering their disappointment at parting.

"Since everything is winding up and you'll be proceeding with whatever you decide to do with Sunrise Key," Chad said, emitting a long sigh, "I'm going to break with professional ethics just this once and offer a tidbit of advice to the other party — although it may sound like I'm still working one-hundred percent for the other side."

"And what advice is that?" she asked.

"Whatever you want to do with Sunrise Key, I wish you the best for that decision. But keep in mind that if you try to revive it as a business operation and fail, you could be in a sacrifice sale position which could drop the selling price considerably."

She brushed a kiss against Chad's cheek. "Thank you, but I was already painfully aware of that. However, I've decided to give it a try. What's an extra million or two?"

"Good girl!" Wick exclaimed, grabbing her in an exuberant bear hug. "Dennis never wanted those developers to get their bulldozers on this place."

As soon as Wick released her, Chad claimed her in a closer embrace crackling with intimacy. "Good luck, darling! I wish I could help you, but —"

"You have business ethics to consider," she finished for him. "Ethics are even a little bit why I love you."

"Darn," said Wick. "So that's the secret. No wonder I lost out."

"I think you're a lot more ethical than you'd like the world to believe, Mr. Daniel Randall Chadwick," Denyse said.

They all stood up and headed toward Wick's boat which he'd left at the main dock tonight.

Chad and Denyse snuggled together, watching as Wick sailed away, disappearing into the blackness, close to midnight.

Chapter 12

She couldn't decide whether midnight or morning was the worst.

She didn't like falling into a restless, unfulfilled sleep alone in her double bed, but she didn't like waking up without Chad beside her either. Like now when the pale light of early sunrise was sneaking into her cottage bedroom, reminding her she was the only occupant.

At least we're apart only sixty-five percent of the week, she consoled herself. She hadn't forgotten those first couple of insecure weeks when she wasn't sure she'd ever have any time with Chad. Once in awhile, some of those old doubts and questions welled up, but the depth of the passion and love he'd shown her for the ensuing two months had calmed most of her fears.

They were honoring their plans for personal time together every weekend, when a hint of anything connected with business was taboo from six P.M. Friday to six A.M. Monday. Chad didn't come to Sunrise Key, saying he would be following her business progress and assessing her probable willingness to sell in all the ways he would usually employ, since he had an obligation to his client. But he wouldn't use his relationship with her to get a firsthand look at the changes taking place on Sunrise Key.

Usually they spent weekends at Chad's condo on Captiva, getting to know each other better, reveling in each other's presence. Last weekend, they'd taken Porque to Disney World, enjoying it every bit as much as the child. Wick had called and asked if he could send Porque to Sunrise Key for the weekend, saying only nebulously that he had something he had to do. They'd had him put Porque on a plane to Orlando instead.

She'd often wished she could have the benefit of business advice from the man she loved. But that area of her life remained sealed. Though she'd consulted other experts, most of the ideas she was implementing were her own, and she could only hope she wasn't making major mistakes.

A tapping at her door surprised her. There must be some emergency. She scrambled out of bed, pulling on the yellow silk kimono.

She blinked at the sight of Chad. Despite the early hour, he was a little scruffy looking, tidbits of soil clinging to his blue jeans and shirt. Silently he held out a bouquet.

Instead of an array of brilliant flowers, the bouquet he offered was —

"Weeds?" she exclaimed. "An indication of the level of your regard for me?"

"Absolutely." He beamed at her with a cheek-stretching smile.

"You'll excuse me while I don't put them in water."

"Absolutely."

She wrapped her arms around his neck. "I don't know how to thank you for such an unusual token of affection."

"We'll think of something."

She wriggled into his embrace, the weed bouquet temporarily forgotten. "I'm glad you're here. I miss you in the mornings."

"Not at night?" he teased.

"Always — except for thirty-five percent of the week."

"That's what I'm here to tell you. That's over for us."

A chill gripped her, as if an Arctic ice storm had hit Florida. She lingered, savoring the feel of him for a last time, then forced herself to slowly withdraw from him. "Oh, I see," she managed to murmur. "Then the weeds are appropriate." Unwanted soon-to-be-dead things.

"More than you know, my love."

His words somehow penetrated a numb

part of her brain. "Your love?" she repeated dumbly.

"Maybe not," he kidded. "You don't seem too articulate in the morning. I might have to reconsider loving you."

"Maybe I just need a good whiff of weeds to get me going."

"That's right. These are for you." He bowed formally, presenting her with the unique botanical arrangement, dirt hanging in clumps where the weeds had been pulled out by their roots.

She accepted them, truly speechless but not for the usual reasons.

"Am I correct in assuming that you don't intend to enshrine those in a crystal vase?" he teased.

"I can't recall seeing any vases around here, crystal or otherwise."

"Then it's okay if you toss them instead." He pulled her into an open area beyond the door. When she didn't respond, he held her arm with his hand and guided it in a throwing motion. "The general idea is to let go."

"Chad, what are you doing? If I scatter weeds, they'll take seed everywhere."

"Just do it," he insisted.

Mildly exasperated but eager to get rid of the disgusting, scratchy bouquet, she gave it a toss. The flimsy weeds separated and fell to the ground less than a yard away.

"I think you'll have to do better than that. I'll pick you some more weeds so you can practice."

"I'm only inarticulate in the morning. You're totally bananas."

"Bananas. There's an idea. Maybe a bunch of bananas would have the right weight to practice with."

"Practice with?" She couldn't help returning his infectious grin.

"Throwing the bouquet. For our wedding, darling!" He gathered her enthusiastically in his arms, spinning her around.

Several deep kisses intervened before she replied aloud, "There's nothing I'd like more than to marry you. But we can't as long as there's a conflict of interest."

"It was very hard to keep worrying about a conflict of interest when only one interest filled every thought, so I got rid of the conflict so I could concentrate on the interest. You."

"But you said you couldn't resign as the buyer's representative for the real estate syndicate because they were such an important client for the firm, not only on this but other projects, and that would affect the firm's worth and Nicole's and Ramon's profits as well."

"All taken care of. I sold my share in the partnership to another well-qualified real estate specialist, with Nicole's and Ramon's agreement. Someone Nicole used to work with. We signed the papers late last night."

"Darling, that's wonderful!" Then she realized how selfish her joy was. "Actually, it's not so wonderful. I didn't want you to give up anything for me, certainly not your career."

"I'm not giving up. I'm getting," he told her softly, "if your answer is yes."

"Yes," she said promptly, taking care of that small matter.

"I still have my career. I'm merely changing my business focus. For now, I'd like to help you if I can. You don't know how hard it's been for me to know you were struggling with all your business decisions alone, capable as you are of making them. I thought pulling some weeds was a good start. Of course, I'll do whatever you say — make the beds —"

"Only mine," she interrupted.

"Mow the grass, scrub the floors, comb the beach."

"So you do have abilities beyond weed pulling?" She feigned a cool, professional tone.

"I do."

"Oh, that sounded very good. Keep practicing that."

"Speaking of practicing —"

"One can never get too much rehearsal."

"I've been replaying this fantasy about you on the beach at sunrise for two months now."

"Carlos, Consuela, and Jacques don't get up this early. And the dayworkers won't be here for hours."

His smile would have set ladies swooning in the aisles at a movie theater.

"Am I by any chance wearing my wanton wench outfit in this fantasy rerun?"

"The outfit is wench. The woman inside it is wanton."

"Very." Already, she was sizzling with desire. She went back into the cottage. "Well, I suppose I have to dress in something."

"Only temporarily."

"By the way," she finally remembered to ask, "I never did find out how you knew about Dressed for Excess and happened to do your shopping there." Even now, she wasn't sure she wanted to know.

"I was their real estate rep when the chain was looking to lease retail space here," he said blankly. "I hear it's doing well."

"If the store is doing as well as the lady

inside its merchandise, it must be soaring."

They started toward the beach, carrying a couple of blankets.

"I'm sorely tempted," Chad said, "and I do mean sorely, not to make it all the way to the beach. Maybe you'd better update me on what's happening with your plans to revive the resort."

"How can I be sure you're not one of the enemy still? A spy," she kidded him. "I happen to know you have excellent qualifications as a male Mata Hari."

"Thank you. But my qualifications in that regard are quickly getting out of hand, so you'll have to take my word that I've defected."

"That makes you a defector, not a defective, right?"

"If we don't hurry to the far end of the beach, I may demonstrate right here how undefective I am."

"Well, in that case, getting down to business, I don't know how much you already know from your usual sources of information."

"Probably all of it. But tell me everything just in case."

"You know we're running day tours from Fort Myers with Carlos bringing small groups of people in the motorboat and noontime picnics on the beach; that provides a little pocket money and helps to get the resort known for when we fully open. People seem to enjoy Clayton and his roommates, and vice versa."

Chad already knew that Sunrise Key was on its way to becoming a new type of sanctuary, for orphaned animals. Clayton's home was shared by another raccoon, a rabbit, and a Key deer fawn found wandering near the highway in Key Largo. A few other orphaned or injured animals were in adjoining, spacious enclosures paralleling their natural habitats. Word had spread quickly about Sunrise Key's availability and willingness to accept orphaned animals through no particular efforts on Sunrise Key's part, and a zoologist and veterinarian were donating time as needed.

She continued, "To raise immediate cash, I'm selling about a third of the existing units on a time-sharing ownership concept where the buyers actually do own, and may occupy it for any month of the year they choose, or trade shorter periods with other buyers. Most of the other units will be rented nightly, like any other resort, and I already have advance bookings for small tour groups. One of my focuses is specialty marketing, both for small tour groups and for individuals."

"Sounds great, so far," he commented.

"A few units are being set aside at low cost where persons with environmental illness can come for long periods of recuperation, or for short vacations in a safe environment. The air here is pure, as you know. Dennis never sprayed chemicals, and I'm not going to. Any renovation of those units will be with hypoallergenic materials. I'm consulting a baubiologist on that —"

"A what?"

"I see there was something you didn't know yet," she said triumphantly. "A baubiologist specializes in the biology of buildings, using ecologically safe materials; natural full spectrum lighting, proper ventilation and air filtration, that kind of thing. There's even such a thing as sick building syndrome. They're finding links between that and all kinds of illnesses and allergies. The only person who can't come to Sunrise Key are those with serious allergies to molds, which of course can't be totally avoided in this climate. Molds are in the soil, everywhere."

"When I said I wanted to be updated on business, I didn't exactly have mold in mind," Chad said with a chuckle. "I don't want to divert my mind too far from our ultimate goal." He added, "But your ideas are terrific."

They entered the edge of the beach, walking as swiftly as their embracing postures and the thick sand would permit, toward the far end to insure privacy.

"You probably know or have guessed at the rest," Denyse continued. "Pretty basic stuff. I sold my condo in Boston, so my money from that equity is providing cash for some paint and supplies to start renovating. The district attorney has agreed that any assets of Burt's belong to the resort as restitution, up to the amount he embezzled. It looks like the sale of his condo, car, furniture, etcetera, won't be nearly enough, but it's a good-sized chunk of money."

"I can offer you another good-sized chunk."

"I'm planning on it," she said with a seductive smile.

"Not that, wanton wench." He feigned insult. "I mean a chunk of money. Besides having already been independently rather wealthy, I now have funds from the sale of my share of the partnership burning a hole in my pocket."

"Is that all it is?" she teased him, even as desire was circuiting its demands through her. "Seriously," she said, "I appreciate your interest in buying in. But I'd still like to keep business and personal matters separate, sort of. I'd appreciate your advice, but this is a challenge I want to see if I can handle on my own without turning to my husband for cash."

"Husband. That sounds marvelous on your lips."

"Your lips on mine would be even more marvelous, future husband."

He obliged, pressing his lips against hers with a demand that made her so weak in the knees she could scarcely stand.

So she stopped trying to stand. They sunk into the sand together.

His hands were already removing the outfit he'd requested she wear. She was undressing him with equal fervor.

Soon their naked lengths were matched, as they knelt in the welcoming sand. Chad cupped her breasts, then lifted them from underneath toward his descending mouth. The tips reacted immediately, radiating warmth through her, with a responding tender knotting at her core.

She leaned into him, alternately breathing hard and forgetting to breathe at all. His hands caressed her, cradled her, stroked her, fondled her into a frenzy.

She welcomed the demanding feel of him against her. He paused only long enough to spread one of the blankets and lower her onto it.

"I love you," he said.

"You take the words right out of my mouth."

"I'll try." He probed her mouth with his tongue, and she likewise searched his.

His gentle penetration seared her soul. The sands beneath reshaped to fit her form, shifting sensuously beneath the blanket, as each of his long, hard thrusts reverberated through her.

Tiny sunbursts exploded along her veins. Then a single bright blazing light commanded the horizon, blocking out everything except the beloved man who brought her to it and shared it with her, as he always would.

The wedding was held on that same beach less than a week later. Wick and Porque came from New Orleans, and Denyse's mother, stepfather, and grandparents came from Boston.

Carlos, Consuela, Jacques, Nicole, and Ramon completed the limited guest list.

Denyse's grandfather had grouched a bit about the early hour. But Denyse and Chad had always known that sunrise was their time.

The start of a new day. The start of a new life.

We hope you have enjoyed this Large Print book. Other Thorndike Press or Chivers Press Large Print books are available at your library or directly from the publishers.

For more information about current and upcoming titles, please call or write, without obligation, to:

Thorndike Press
295 Kennedy Memorial Drive
Waterville, ME 04901 USA
Tel. (800) 223-1244

OR

Chivers Press Limited
Windsor Bridge Road
Bath BA2 3AX
England
Tel. (0225) 335336

All our Large Print titles are designed for easy reading, and all our books are made to last.